Fabulous Fathers

"I have to do this.... My children need me,"

Derek insisted. He took a deep breath and merged with Jeffrey Callander's body. It was an eerie experience. He couldn't even find words to describe it. But it worked—he was inside! He was alive again!

"Doctor! He's opening his eyes—my God, he's opening his eyes!"

The woman's voice startled Derek. He blinked—and found himself looking up at the gorgeous redhead through Jeffrey Callander's eyes. She was crying.

"He's awake," she sobbed. "It's a miracle!"

Then she lowered her face to his and kissed him tenderly.

And Derek wondered what he'd gotten himself into.

Dear Reader,

Celebration 1000! continues in May with more wonderful books by authors you've loved for years and so many of your new favorites!

Starting with . . . *The Best Is Yet To Be* by Tracy Sinclair. Bride-to-be Valentina Richardson finally meets Mr. Right. Too bad he's her fiancé's best friend!

Favorite author Marie Ferrarella brings us BABY'S CHOICE—an exciting new series where matchmaking babies bring their unsuspecting parents together!

The FABULOUS FATHERS continue with Derek Wolfe, a *Miracle Dad*. A fanciful and fun-filled romance from Toni Collins.

This month we're very pleased to present our *debut* author, Carolyn Zane, with her first book, *The Wife Next Door*. In this charming, madcap romance, neighbors David Barclay and Lauren Wills find that make-believe marriage can lead to the real thing!

Carol Grace brings us a romantic contest of wills in the *The Lady Wore Spurs*. And don't miss *Race to the Altar* by Patricia Thayer.

In June and July, look for more exciting Celebration 1000! books by Debbie Macomber, Elizabeth August, Annette Broadrick and Laurie Paige. We've planned this event for you, our wonderful readers. So, stake out your favorite easy chair and get ready to fall in love all over again with Silhouette Romance.

Happy reading!

Anne Canadeo
Senior Editor
Silhouette Romance

Please address questions and book requests to:
Reader Service
U.S.: P.O. Box 1325, Buffalo, NY 14269
Canadian: P.O. Box 1050, Niagara Falls, Ont. L2E 7G7

MIRACLE DAD
Toni Collins

Silhouette
ROMANCE™
Published by Silhouette Books
America's Publisher of Contemporary Romance

For Dad, Tony and Bugsy,
who are no doubt turning
Heaven upside down themselves.

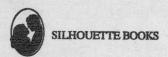 SILHOUETTE BOOKS

ISBN 0-373-19008-5

MIRACLE DAD

Copyright © 1994 by Toni Collins

This edition published by arrangement with Harlequin Enterprises B.V.

® and TM are trademarks of Harlequin Enterprises B.V., used under license. Trademarks indicated with ® are registered in the United States Patent and Trademark Office, the Canadian Trade Marks Office and in other countries.

Printed in U.S.A.

TONI COLLINS

is a bestselling author of mainstream novels under her real name. She has worked in numerous occupations, all with one goal in mind: to one day realize her dream of being a full-time writer.

When Ms. Collins began writing for Silhouette Books, she felt a greater freedom with the category romance format, since she felt that she "could do things in these books that simply didn't fit" her mainstream books.

Ms. Collins has traveled extensively and now lives in St. Louis with her son.

Derek Wolfe on Fatherhood . . .

Patrick and Alexandra, after your mother left, I worried that you might not ever get over it, that no matter what I did, it might not be enough—but we did okay, didn't we? We were a family, a real family, at least until I had to leave you. I didn't want to. I hope you both knew that. Love is the one thing you *can* take with you into the next life, and it was my love for the two of you that enabled me to come back, to make sure that Evelyn was indeed the right woman to be your new mother. How could I have known then that she would be the right woman for *all* of us? You'll never know how much I've wanted to tell you the truth, to let you know that I'm back, that we can be a family again, the two of you, and me—and Evelyn. But even though I can't, I think that somehow you *do* know, that you can feel it even if you can't see it or hear it. I have to believe that, because I know now that love crosses all boundaries. . . .

Chapter One

Derek Wolfe still couldn't believe it, even after six Earth months. He was really in Heaven! This came as quite a surprise to him, since he hadn't exactly been a believer while he was among the living. "We've had to lower our standards in the past century," Michael, one of the senior angels, had admitted to Derek with a heavy sigh of resignation shortly after Derek's arrival. "Otherwise, we'd end up with embarrassingly few new admissions. It would be humiliating to have the southern team end up with everybody."

"So I got in by default," Derek had concluded.

Michael had nodded. If angels could blush, he probably would have. But then, Michael did not look much like an angel—at least he didn't look the way angels looked in books and paintings. He was small—short and very thin—with shaggy brown hair and a beard, square, granny glasses, faded jeans, a white T-shirt bearing the Nike slogan Just Do It, and he spoke with a heavy New England accent. Was Heaven regional? Derek didn't know. There was a lot he didn't yet know about Heaven, but then he hadn't been here long. All he knew at this moment was that he—with his ash-blond hair and blue eyes and toothpaste smile—looked more like an angel than Michael did.

"That's about the size of it." Michael was responding to his question about default.

Derek frowned. "I guess I should consider myself lucky, then."

"Very," Michael agreed with a nod. "You know how unbearable the heat can be without central airconditioning," he pointed out.

Derek appreciated Michael's sense of humor. The few times on Earth he had actually thought about Heaven, wondered if it existed at all, he'd never thought of it as a funny place. Or angels as funny—beings.

Derek could have been happy here. It was an incredible place—perfect in every way. The sun was always shining, the birds were always singing, the flowers were always in full bloom. Everyone was always happy, and there was no pain or sadness or disappointment. Yes, Derek thought, I could be very happy here.

If it weren't for his children.

His wife of five years had walked out on him and their two children to "find herself" professionally. Patrick had been four then and Alexandra two. In two years, Patricia had made no attempt to see them or even find out if they were all right. Then, suddenly, she was gone, killed in a plane crash. Six months later, he was dead, too, and Patrick and Alexandra were in a foster home—a temporary arrangement at best— facing an uncertain future.

Derek wanted better than that for his kids. He talked to them when they were alone, usually at night, trying to reassure them, but he couldn't get used to the idea that he could no longer hold them, hug them, physically comfort them as he'd always done before.

He couldn't get used to being dead.

He hadn't even realized he was dead—at first. It had all happened so fast. One minute he was jogging down a quiet street not far from home, as he had every morning since they'd moved into that house. Then there was a sudden, sharp pain, like a sharp blow to his entire body, and he found himself having an out-of-body experience, floating in the air, looking down at the paramedics who were trying to save his life. He hadn't even seen the truck that hit him. Now that he thought about it, he couldn't even remember feeling very much pain beyond that initial blow. But there must have been pain—the truck tossed him twenty feet into the air, according to the driver who described the accident to the policemen on the scene.

He frowned. The real pain, the lingering pain, had been Patrick and Alexandra's . . . and there wasn't a thing he could do to help them. Why hadn't he seen through Patricia? Why had he married such a cold, unfeeling woman? His heart ached for his children, for the pain his death—and Patricia's indifference—had caused them. If only he could hold them, tell them everything would be all right—but he couldn't and it wouldn't.

Not ever again.

"Has anybody ever gone back?" Derek asked Michael.

If the senior angel was surprised by the question, he was doing a first-rate job of hiding it. "All the time," he answered without hesitation. "Surely you've heard of reincarnation."

Derek nodded. "Heard of it, yes—believed in it, no," he admitted.

Michael frowned. "You didn't believe in much of anything when you were alive, did you?" he observed solemnly.

"I believed in myself," Derek responded with a shrug.

"What about your children, your family? What about *love*, Derek?" Michael wanted to know.

Derek shot him an indignant look. "Of course I did! What kind of a man do you think I am—was?"

"A wounded one," Michael answered honestly, seriously. "Growing up in a broken home, you wouldn't have had much exposure to things like love, affection, trust or faith."

"The Four Horsemen of the Apocalypse," Derek said with unmasked sarcasm.

"Watch the blasphemy there, Wolfe," Michael cautioned him. "The Boss doesn't like that sort of thing, you know."

Derek opened his mouth to ask how Michael had known about the orphanage, but then it hit him. Of course he knew. These guys knew everything. "What was your life on Earth like, Mike?" he asked in a bid to change the subject. His own childhood memories weren't pleasant ones.

"I was with Greenpeace," Michael told him. "And don't call me Mike."

"Greenpeace, huh? Save the Earth and all that?"

"Something like that, yes. I was a crusader, always the champion of the underdog. I suppose because I'd grown up an underdog myself."

"Oh, yeah?"

Michael nodded. "I got picked on a lot as a kid—always attracted the neighborhood bullies. So, when I grew up, I was always looking out for those who couldn't defend themselves."

"Like the whales and the baby seals."

Michael winced. "That's how I died."

"Saving the whales?"

He shook his head. "Baby seals. The hunters would come onto shore and club them to death," he recalled. "I was part of a group trying to stop them. I got clubbed instead."

"I'm sorry."

"I'm not." Michael paused for just a moment. "But we were talking about you. Even after you grew up, and became a marketing executive, you remained a loner, for the most part," he continued, "until you became a father. That was the turning point in your life."

"It sure has—it sure was," Derek recalled, smiling at the memory. "They taught me how to love."

Michael shook his head, clucking disapprovingly. "And having experienced something so miraculous, still you had no faith."

Derek was growing even more uncomfortable and even more determined to change the subject. "About this reincarnation business . . ." he started.

Michael smiled knowingly. "Oh, yes. I take it you have little knowledge of the—ah—process."

"Down there, everybody's got a different theory," Derek told him. "Hard to tell which one's the right one—if indeed any of them are."

Michael sucked in a deep breath. "Well, basically, what happens is that one must be born again—literally," he began. "The party returning to the living would return as a newborn—a baby, or perhaps an animal."

"An animal!"

Michael shrugged. "Any port in a storm," he pointed out.

"That wouldn't work," Derek said, shaking his head.

Michael looked at him. "Wouldn't work for whom?" he asked.

Derek didn't respond to the question. "Nothing. Just a thought," he said evasively, knowing even as he did that Michael was probably reading his thoughts and knew exactly what he had in mind. "Isn't there any other way to do it?"

"Any other way to go back, you mean?" Michael nodded. "Just one."

"How?"

"A body without a soul."

Derek gave him a puzzled look. "I don't understand...." he began.

"Of course you don't," Michael said patiently. "You haven't been one of us long enough. A body without a soul is one being kept alive by artificial means. The soul has already passed into our dimension, but the body is still being kept functional in their world."

"One on life support," Derek concluded.

Michael nodded again. "Most—but not all—of these souls have completely abandoned their Earthly shells."

"The body is uninhabited."

"Crude, but basically correct," Michael conceded.

Derek nodded, too. That made sense, in a crazy kind of way. "Sort of like vacancies at the motel."

Michael rolled his eyes upward. "Must you always be so graphic?" he asked, exasperated.

"Sorry," Derek apologized. "Old habits are as hard as h—are hard to break."

"It's not an easy thing to do, you know—finding a body without a soul," Michael told him.

"Maybe not," Derek responded, "but I'd like to try."

"In your case, I wouldn't recommend it," Michael said honestly.

"Why not in my case?"

Michael sighed heavily. "If you're going to force me to be blunt, Derek, you barely met the requirements to get here. If you go back and—if you'll pardon the expression—screw up, you'll never get in again."

Derek frowned. It was risky, all right. But this was a risk he had to take.

His kids needed him.

"Well, then," Michael said in a resigned tone, "we do have one candidate who would be perfect...."

Evelyn Sloan was exhausted. Running her own restaurant—even with her sister helping—wasn't easy. She would have liked nothing better than to go home, take a long, hot bath and spend the evening curled up with a good book—but she knew it wasn't going to be that way. Her already long day was far from over.

With two small children waiting for her at home, it wasn't likely she'd get that well-deserved rest until they were in bed and sound asleep.

Evelyn smiled to herself. Even at times like this, when it would be easier to be single and childless, she loved being a foster mother and hoped to make the arrangement a permanent one. She parked her car in the driveway and directed her gaze toward the front door. Predictably, it flew open and seven-year-old Patrick and five-year-old Alexandra emerged, racing toward the car as they did every night when she came home.

"Hi, guys!" she greeted as she got out of the car. They clutched her hands as they all walked back to the house together, chattering happily.

It wasn't always like this, Evelyn thought. When they first came to live with her five months ago, both children had been depressed and emotionally withdrawn. They'd wanted no part of her. Winning them over hadn't been easy, but she'd refused to give up on them—and eventually, it had paid off.

Still, they had their days. Anything that reminded them of their father brought a quiet response from the children—and there were a lot of things that reminded them of their father. Like that early summer Sunday they'd spent at the Seattle zoo....

"Daddy used to bring us to the zoo a lot," Patrick remembered. "We'd bring a lunch—a big lunch—and we'd sit on a blanket over by the big pond and watch the ducks while we ate."

Evelyn thought of the wicker picnic hamper full of sandwiches and snacks in the trunk of her car and wondered if it might not be a better idea to take the children to a fast-food place for lunch instead. Daddy, she decided, was tough competition.

She finally decided they would eat their picnic lunch by the pond as she had planned. She told herself she couldn't go on avoiding anything and everything that reminded the children of their father. It wasn't possible and it wouldn't do the children any good.

Instead, she encouraged them to talk about their father, to share their memories of him with her. It was rough at first—but after a while, she could see that it was helping them to deal with their loss. It also helped her to learn about the life they'd had before their father's death....

"Could we rent some videos tonight?" Patrick was asking as Evelyn opened the front door.

Evelyn smiled wryly. "What did you have in mind?" she asked. As if she didn't already know.

"The Land Before Time!" Patrick responded enthusiastically.

"Beauty and the Beast!" Alexandra cried.

Patrick looked at Evelyn hopefully. "Both?" he asked.

Evelyn pretended to be considering the proposition. "Did either of you give Betty any trouble today?" she wanted to know.

"No!" they chorused.

She gave them a knowing smile. "You're sure about that?" she asked.

"Absolutely," Alexandra insisted.

"Ask Betty if you don't believe us," Patrick suggested.

Patrick knew, as well as Evelyn did, that her mother, who came by to look after them while Evelyn was at work, would never snitch on them. "One of these days, she's going to fool you and spill the beans," Evelyn warned.

Patrick wrinkled his nose disdainfully. "Spill the—what?" he asked.

"Never mind." With Patrick and Alexandra following closely behind Evelyn headed for the kitchen, where her mother was preparing dinner. "These two give you any trouble today, Mom?" she asked, selecting an apple from a basket of fresh fruit on the counter.

"Not at all," the older woman assured her.

"You wouldn't be covering for them, would you?"

Betty Sloan shot her daughter a disapproving look. "Such a suspicious daughter I've raised," she declared, sending the kids off to watch TV, armed with cookies and milk.

"I'm not suspicious, I just know you," Evelyn said, taking a bite of the apple. "They have you wrapped around their little fingers."

"And not you?" Betty looked skeptical. "You've bent over backward trying to replace their father."

"Replace their father?" Evelyn's laugh was hollow. "Their father's a tough act to follow. A real Superdad."

"The kind of man you should be looking for now that you're free of that no-account Jeffrey Callander," her mother pointed out.

Evelyn frowned. Under the circumstances, she doubted she and her former fiancé would ever have had a future together.

She doubted now that Jeffrey would have a future at all.

Evelyn had been lucky by anyone's standards. She'd grown up in a happy, secure home with two parents who had a good, solid marriage, who loved each other and their two daughters. Sharon used to call them "the perfect TV family," and even though she'd been joking, it was very close to the truth. Theirs was the kind of family most kids only wished they had. Evelyn and Sharon had been brought up to think for themselves, to believe in themselves. Individuality had been strongly encouraged. Self-confidence came to them as naturally as breathing. Evelyn had always known that one day she'd have a family of her own, just like the one in which she'd grown up.

Then she met Jeffrey Callander.

Jeffrey had exploded into her life, quite literally, at a time when she'd been looking for fun more than anything else, and Jeffrey had provided that and more. They'd had an extraordinary romance—but when the party was over, as Sharon had so aptly put it, they hadn't had the staying power to make it for the long haul, to get them through those inevitable tough times. Jeffrey, unlike Evelyn, *hadn't* grown up in a warm, loving, stable home and was a real skeptic when it came to long-term relationships. But Evelyn had glimpsed a side of him he seldom allowed anyone to see, and she'd convinced herself he had the potential—and the desire—to change.

How wrong she'd been.

Evelyn had taken a long look at herself and what she found important and decided to do something about it. Gradually she stopped looking for just the fun things in life and began to discover what she really wanted.

Seeing a segment on the local TV news about children needing foster parents, Evelyn's heart went out to those youngsters who didn't have a home of any

kind to call their own. She decided to look into the
foster-parents program in her area, to see if a single
woman could qualify as a foster parent. She was assured that she would—but she was also cautioned that
it would be difficult for her to formally adopt her foster child, so it would not be wise for her to become too
attached to any child she brought into her home. Evelyn wasn't worried. She and Jeffrey would marry
soon, and two parents with a six-figure income would
certainly have a good shot at being approved.

Her mother was worried about her. Betty Sloan
knew only too well how warm and open, how giving
of herself, her daughter was. Betty also knew that,
while single parents did adopt children these days, it
was still the exception rather than the rule. And her
fiancé would want no part of such a proposition, no
matter how sure Evelyn was that he would "come
around." Jeffrey Callander simply did not want children—his own or anyone else's.

That proved to be a textbook understatement. Jeffrey had been furious with Evelyn for making such an
important decision—one that would affect both of
them—without even discussing it with him. Evelyn
had been stunned that he could feel as he did about it.
They'd argued for weeks, with Jeffrey going out of his
way to avoid spending any time with the two children
she'd brought into her home. That was when Evelyn's feelings for Jeffrey began to change, when she
decided not to marry him.

She broke the engagement the night before his accident—an accident for which she blamed herself. If
she hadn't broken it off with him, maybe he wouldn't
have gone diving that morning—or if he had, he
would have been paying more attention to safety pre-

cautions. If, if... Now, with Jeffrey's life hanging in the balance, she promised him, promised herself, that if he survived, she would make it up to him.

Somehow.

"I want to go on the record as being against this." Michael pleaded to the heavens as he followed Derek down the bustling hospital corridor. Thank God no one could see them.

"This way," Derek directed, heading into the intensive-care unit. This was a real hoot, being able to walk through walls or anything else he chose; being able to fly and self-levitate and do all kinds of other things he couldn't do as a flesh-and-blood man.

"This isn't a magic show," Michael reprimanded him. "Stop showing off."

"How can I be showing off?" Derek challenged. "No one can see me!"

Of course, there *were* limitations, even for angels. There were always limitations. There were things, important things, that mortal men could do, but Heavenly spirits couldn't. And those were the things Derek found himself missing most.

Careful there, he cautioned himself. Michael can read your mind.

They checked out every room in the ICU. "This is Mollie McFadden," Michael explained as they stood over an elderly woman who was very near death. "She'll be joining us within the hour." He looked at Derek questioningly.

Derek shook his head. "It has to be a man's body," he insisted.

"Picky, picky, picky," Michael clucked. "Oh, very well—shall we move on?"

"Good idea."

In the next room was a middle-aged man on life support. "His name is George Marsden." Michael introduced the man as if he were awake and could hear them. "He was in an auto accident. He actually left this world days ago, but his family refuses to let him go without a fight."

Derek grimaced. "Too old."

Michael was exasperated. "Well, excuse me, pal, but Kevin Costner's body isn't available at the moment," he snapped irritably.

"I'm not *that* picky, Mike."

"I'm beginning to wonder. And don't call me Mike."

Derek looked around. "Any more candidates?"

"You make this sound like a beauty pageant," Michael snorted as he started off. "But there *is* another man who'd be perfect for what you have in mind. Follow me."

They entered another room, where a man who appeared to be about Derek's age was being kept alive—physically—by a myriad of machines. "This is Jeffrey Callander," Michael told him. "Age thirty-five, single—for the moment—comes from a filthy rich family, has a nice, fat bank account of his own and is quite easy on the eyes. If he doesn't meet your needs, I suggest we pack it in and go home."

"What happened to him?" Derek asked, looking down at the other man thoughtfully.

"He's something of a daredevil, I'm afraid—likes to take chances," Michael said with a disapproving shake of his head. "Skydiving, polo, water sports— you name it. He went diving in Puget Sound once too often."

"Head injury?" Derek asked.

Michael shook his head again. "Oxygen-tank malfunction. He was without air too long."

Derek frowned. "He's already—" He found himself curiously unable to say the word. *Dead*.

"His soul crossed over days ago," Michael said quietly, folding his arms across his chest. "He doesn't have any family to make the decision to let his body go, and the lawyers are still arguing about what to do. There's no one who really cares for him. Except her." He nodded toward an attractive redhead at Jeffrey's side, clutching his hand, willing him to come back to her.

"Who's that?" Derek asked, thinking the woman looked vaguely familiar.

"His former fiancée, Evelyn Sloan. Lovely, isn't she?" Michael glanced skyward. "Forgive me for what I'm thinking right now, Boss." He turned back to Derek.

"Former fiancée?"

"Yeah," Michael said with a nod. "Seems Jeffrey didn't want to be a daddy, so when Evelyn brought home two small children who'd just lost their father, Jeffrey was ready to cancel the caterer. Evelyn beat him to it."

Derek was stunned. "Kids? Two kids?"

Michael nodded again. "A boy and a girl. Your children, to be precise. That's why I thought Jeffrey might be right for you."

Derek didn't respond. He was still staring at the woman. Evelyn Sloan. He couldn't believe it. She was the one! *She* was Patrick and Alexandra's foster mother. This was perfect. He looked down at Jeffrey again. "This one should do quite nicely."

"It's a d—a good thing," Michael said with a sigh of relief. "If he hadn't been acceptable, we would have had to go back to puppies or piglets."

"*Piglets?*"

"Squatters can't be choosers, Derek. I've already explained the realities to you."

Derek paused. "Well, then—when can I move in?" he asked.

"Move in? For Heaven's sake—" Michael caught himself and muttered a quick apology to the heavens. "Do you want to sign a lease? Would you like to check it out to see if the neighborhood suits you? Come on, Derek—this isn't a condo we're talking about."

"Well, excuse me—this is all new to me, you know," Derek pointed out.

Michael pursed his lips thoughtfully. "Right. Well, since you must think of this in Earthly terms, you can take possession—if you'll pardon the expression—immediately."

"Like now?" Derek was surprised.

"*Now,*" Michael echoed with emphasis. "You can drive it off the lot—without a warranty, of course. All models are as is."

Try as he sometimes did to hide it, Michael did have a sense of humor, Derek decided. "How do I, uh, do it?" he wanted to know.

Michael rubbed his chin and thought it over momentarily. "To tell you the truth, I'm not exactly sure," he admitted.

"You're not sure?"

"I've never done it before myself—and I've never supervised anyone else dumb enough to try," Michael responded defensively.

"But you're my sponsor—you're supposed to know these things." Derek was near panic.

"Nobody's perfect, Derek," Michael reminded him, looking mildly insulted.

"Aren't angels supposed to be?"

"Close, but not quite. Look at you."

"That was low, Mike."

"I told you not to call me Mike."

"Didn't anyone every call you Mike when you were—alive?" Derek asked, curious.

"Sure. All the time. But that was different."

"Different how?"

"I'm an angel now. I have to be dignified," Michael sniffed.

"You sure don't *look* dignified."

"What do you expect, Saint Peter?"

"At least *he'd* know how to get me in there," Derek said crossly, pointing to Jeffrey.

Michael gave a frustrated gesture. "Why don't you just go in—you know, like walking through a wall, only you don't come out on the other side."

"That sounds stupid."

Now Michael *was* insulted. "Do you have a better idea, Einstein?" he demanded hotly.

"No," Derek admitted.

"Well, then?"

"Oh, I suppose it's worth a try," Derek conceded.

Michael paused. "There are a couple of things I should mention before you, uh, take possession," he said.

"Like what?"

"For one thing, your kids won't know who you are," Michael stated.

"*What?*"

"You're going to be in someone else's body, Derek. You won't look like Derek Wolfe, you'll look like Jeffrey Callander."

"I'll tell *her* who I am."

"Oh, that'll be perfect. She'll think you're a wacko and have you hauled off to a rubber room," Michael predicted. "On Earth, you're dead, remember? How many among the living actually believe it's possible to come back?"

Derek scratched his head, perplexed. "You have a point there."

"Right. Another thing—you have to check in with me from time to time."

"What for?"

"House rules." He pointed upward.

"Just how am I supposed to do that?" Derek asked, confused.

"You can leave the body while it sleeps."

"That's always good to know."

"And one last thing."

"Yeah?"

"This is only temporary."

"Now wait a minute—"

"That's the number-one rule, Derek. The Boss doesn't make exceptions," Michael stressed. "You're dead—your time's up. Jeffrey's dead, too. The body's just a loaner."

Derek hadn't anticipated this. "How long do I have?" he asked carefully.

"Sixty days."

"So, do I get penalized for any days I go over?"

"Definitely. You get booted out of Heaven for eternity."

"Punishment's a little harsh, isn't it?"

"I don't make the rules, I only enforce them," Michael maintained.

Derek took a deep breath. "Well, I guess this is it."

"What are you waiting for?"

"Nothing, I guess." He started forward.

"Wait a minute, Derek."

He stopped in his tracks. "Now what?"

"You're going to be living in Jeffrey's body, which means you will have to live Jeffrey's life. That's not going to be easy, you know."

"Dandy."

"If you want to back out—"

"No way. I have to do this, Mike—Michael," he insisted. "My children need me."

He took a deep breath and merged with Jeffrey Callander's lifeless body. It was an eerie experience—even more so than leaving his own body had been. He couldn't even find words to describe it. But it worked—he was inside! He was alive again!

"Doctor! He's opening his eyes—my God, he's opening his eyes!"

The woman's voice startled Derek. He blinked—and found himself looking up at the gorgeous redhead through Jeffrey Callander's eyes. She was crying.

"He's awake," she sobbed. "It's a miracle!"

Then she lowered her face to his and kissed him tenderly.

And Derek wondered what he'd gotten himself into.

Chapter Two

"It's a miracle, all right," the doctor agreed once he'd finished examining Jeffrey. He removed his stethoscope and shoved it down into the pocket of his white lab coat. "I would have bet he wouldn't have one chance in a thousand of pulling through."

Evelyn smiled, biting her lower lip to keep from crying again. "Will he be all right?" she asked anxiously. "I mean—will he make a full recovery?"

The doctor frowned. "It's too soon to tell, Ms. Sloan," he answered honestly, rubbing his chin as if he were calculating the odds. "He's been in a coma over two months now. It would surprise me greatly if there were no permanent damage."

"By 'permanent damage,' what, exactly, do you mean?" she asked hesitantly. Suddenly her legs felt like jelly.

He shrugged. "It could be any one of a number of things," he said. "He could be paralyzed—totally or partially, depending upon the extent and location of the damage. He could be deaf, or unable to talk. He could lose his sight. Or he could sustain a full or partial memory loss."

"Memory loss?" Evelyn was stunned and unable to hide it, even if she had wanted to. "You mean he might not remember who I am? Who he is?"

The doctor nodded. "I'm sorry to say that's a very real possibility," he acknowledged regretfully.

Evelyn fought back tears. She didn't know what she would do if Jeffrey didn't remember her. She looked down at him, her own trembling hand reaching for his. She was fighting hard, harder than she ever had before, to maintain her self-control. "He's not—he's not in a coma now, is he?" she asked.

The doctor managed a weak smile. "No, my dear," he answered. "He's just sleeping. He'll do a lot of that for a while. His body—and his mind—are very weak. This has been quite stressful for him."

Evelyn was silent for a moment. "Would it be all right if I were to stay with him for a while?" she asked finally. "I'd like to be here when he wakes up."

"Of course." He patted her arm reassuringly. "Stay as long as you like. It will do him—and you—a great deal of good for him to see you when he wakes again."

After the doctor left the room, Evelyn settled down in a chair beside the bed and wept openly. She'd believed the worst was over when he emerged from the coma. She'd been so sure everything was going to be all right. She didn't know what she was going to do if he didn't remember her, didn't remember their life together. It would be devastating enough if he were to be blind or deaf or unable to walk or talk—but to lose his memory. The only thing worse than that would be if he had died. In some ways, it would be as if he *had* died.

Her relationship with Jeffrey had never been an easy one, though she had to admit it had never lacked for excitement. They'd met three years ago at a party. He'd singled her out right away and, like a tidal wave, had swept her off her feet with his charm and wit and his flamboyant, no-holds-barred approach to romance. There was no one like Jeffrey Callander, not before him and never again. He was handsome and witty and had a zest for life that was contagious. He'd thought nothing of flying off with her on his private jet to Barbados or Oahu for a romantic weekend or just to San Francisco for lunch.

Evelyn had loved Jeffrey, and she had always believed he loved her. If she hadn't, she wouldn't have stayed with him as long as she had. He'd always balked at the prospect of marriage. He said he liked things the way they were, that he didn't want their relationship to change, to be ruined. He didn't want to take her for granted. *He* didn't want to be taken for granted.

Evelyn had always suspected his feelings were tied up with the divorce of his own parents when he was young. He believed his parents' marriage had stagnated because they'd come to take each other for granted. His most vivid memories of his mother were of a lonely, desperately unhappy woman who almost never saw her husband when they *were* married, and his memories of his father were precious few—he was usually coming or going, always with a suitcase or briefcase in his hand. His father had been a man who quite literally worked himself to death—which explained Jeffrey's obsession with enjoying life to its fullest, with taking chances, challenging fate in the riskiest of ways. Jeffrey rarely talked about it, but she knew his childhood had been a painfully lonely one. She'd concluded that it was why he was so adamant about not having children of his own.

He'd finally come around on the idea of marriage—they'd gotten engaged eight months ago at Christmas. But as she'd realized what was really important, things had changed. Try as she had to understand him, to deal with the problems she knew were rooted deeply within him, she couldn't accept the idea of never having children, never being a mother. Why couldn't he show some consideration for her feelings, her needs?

But if I hadn't called it off, she thought now, would you be here, like this, fighting for your life?

Derek wondered how much longer he could pretend to be asleep.

He needed time—time to think, time to figure out how he was going to handle this. He knew virtually nothing about Jeffrey Callander *or* Evelyn Sloan. How was he supposed to just assume Jeffrey's identity? How could he possibly pull it off?

Even *he* couldn't bluff his way through this one.

"You're going to have to help me out here, Michael," Derek communicated with the senior angel mentally. *"There's no way I can play this by ear."*

No response.

"Michael?"

"I'm here, Derek—and I'm pleased to know that you can be humble," Michael responded. *"Unfortunately, the information I am able to provide is going to be somewhat limited."*

"I thought you guys were supposed to have all the answers."

Michael gave a heavy sigh. *"We've been through all of this before, Derek."*

"All right, all right. Just give me what you have, then."

"As you go along, pal. As you go along."

"You're a big help."

"We try."

"What am I supposed to do, fake it?"

"Don't be silly. All you have to do is listen to your heart, Derek. It will tell you which way to go."

"I never thought of you as a romantic, Michael."

"Being an angel, it's hard not to be."

"So, where do I go from here?"

"Waking up would be a fine start."

"You're about as funny as a traffic accident."

"I wasn't trying to be funny, Derek. I was simply being practical. You can't get this rolling until you take that first step."

"Right. Thanks."

"Don't mention it."

"Over and out." Then, after a pause, *"Michael?"*

No response.

"Michael!"

Still no response.

I guess this means I'm on my own, Derek thought miserably. He felt like he'd just bailed out of a jet at thirty-five-thousand feet without a parachute. His mind was racing, trying to figure out how he was going to handle this. How was he going to deal with Evelyn? This man had been her fiancé, for crying out loud. She probably knew everything about him.

Or maybe not. He'd been married to Patricia for five years and discovered he really hadn't known her at all.

I could fake amnesia, he told himself. Didn't the doctor tell Evelyn that Jeffrey could have lost his memory?

A total memory loss. That's the ticket.

Then he reconsidered. No, what won't work. How can I possibly get close to her if I don't even remember her? Or my own identity?

No good, no good at all. Think, Wolfe.

Partial amnesia—yeah, that's it.

I can remember her, but not be able to remember everything. That would cover my goofs. In fact, she can help me remember. Yeah, that'll bring us even closer together.

"Derek!"

"Oh, hi, Michael."

"We're watching you, Derek. Remember that."

"Thanks for reminding me."

"That's what senior angels are for."

Derek opened his eyes—Jeffrey's eyes—slowly, smiling up at Evelyn. "Hi there, beautiful," he said in a weak voice that startled him, until he realized he was speaking with Jeffrey's voice now, not his own.

Her head jerked as if he'd taken her by surprise. "Jeffrey," she gasped. "You're—"

"Alive and kickin', honey." He grinned. "Miss me?"

"Jeffrey!" She started to sob uncontrollably.

"Why are you crying?" he asked seriously. "Didn't you want me to pull through?"

"Don't be silly!" She was laughing and crying at the same time, wiping her tears away as best she could with a wad of tissues that was already soaked. "I'm just happy, that's all."

"Yeah, you look happy." His tone was mildly teasing as he reached out to take her hand. This new body was going to take some getting used to. It felt different in every way. It was like a new pair of shoes that didn't quite fit and weren't as comfortable as a favorite pair of worn-out sneakers.

"I *am* happy," she assured him. "Oh, Jeffrey, I was so afraid you wouldn't make it."

"Never!" he snorted.

Her tears flowed freely now. "The doctors kept saying you wouldn't make it, that you were brain-dead...."

He made a face and found that it hurt. Actually, there wasn't much that didn't hurt at the moment. "No big deal," he told her. "Lots of people get along just fine without brains."

"Jeffrey!" Evelyn laughed as she stroked his hair with her free hand. "I see you haven't lost your wit."

At least I got one thing right, Derek thought. That's a step in the right direction. What's that saying? Every journey begins with a single step. Yeah, that's it. I don't remember who said it, but I hope he knew what he was talking about. Aloud he asked, "How long have I been, uh—you know—"

She looked puzzled for a moment. "You mean in a coma?" she asked when it finally dawned on her. "Two months and a few days."

Two months!

This guy should be shriveled up like a raisin, Derek thought. No wonder his body feels funny. It shrunk. "I feel like Rip Van Winkle," he told Evelyn.

She wiped her eyes again, this time using one corner of the sheet covering him. "I wish they'd bring in another box of tissues," she said, her voice trembling as much as her hands.

"Want me to ring for the nurse?" he asked.

She shook her head emphatically. "No. Not yet," she said. "It's been two months since we've been together, really together, or had any time alone. I want to be alone with you for a while now."

"Me, too," he said, not knowing what else to say and trying to figure out how he could ask about his kids.

She pulled herself together as best she could. "As crazy as this is going to sound, I can't tell you what I'm really feeling right now," she confessed. "I'm still numb. This has been a nightmare, a terrible nightmare, and until today, I was terrified I wasn't ever going to wake up from it. I'd resigned myself to the probability that you weren't going to make it. Everyone—all of the doctors, the specialists—said you wouldn't. They said over and over again that there was no chance, absolutely no chance." She started to cry once more.

"Honey, don't cry. It's going to be all right. Uh, I do have to say I've forgotten a lot, though. I remember my name, and yours, and that we're engaged, but the rest is a blur."

"You mean you don't remember—" Evelyn stopped speaking before she could say she'd broken their engagement. She didn't want to upset him, so she decided she wouldn't say anything until his memory came back. Her tears began to flow again.

Derek's heart went out to Evelyn in a way that surprised him. He wished he knew more about her relationship with this guy. Was it a good one? Did Callander treat her well? Did he deserve this woman, or was he a real cad? Were they planning a wedding in the near future?

"Michael, I think we need to talk... Now!"

"Do you remember the Barf Inn?" Evelyn asked as she fed him breakfast two mornings later. She was always there at mealtimes, always insisting upon feeding him even though the nurses insisted he could do it himself. She wanted to do these things for him, needed to do them. She couldn't explain how, but doing little things for him gave her peace, satisfaction.

"The what?" he asked, a look of total confusion on his pallid face, a face that in the past, had always been tanned and reflecting good health.

She laughed. "I'm glad you're not a restaurant critic," she said, gently wiping his mouth and chin. "I'd already be out of business."

"You own it?" he asked.

Evelyn nodded. "I'm co-owner with my sister, Sharon," she explained. "Do you remember Sharon?"

He shook his head.

"That should make you very happy," she said in a half-joking tone. "The two of you have been making a monumental effort to forget each other's existence since the day I introduced you."

"We didn't get along?" he asked, puzzled.

She laughed heartily. "To say that you and Sharon didn't get along is like describing World War II as a minor peace disturbance."

"Why?"

"Why what?" She turned her attention back to his breakfast to let him know she didn't want to discuss it further.

"Why didn't we get along?" He wanted to know, or rather he *needed* to know. He needed to know as much as possible.

She really did not want to get into this with him. Not now. Maybe not ever. "Why do any two people not get along?" she asked, keeping her tone light. "Personalities clash...."

His eyes met hers. "There's more to it than that, isn't there?"

She looked down at the plate, avoiding his eyes. Finally she nodded.

He reached out to her. "Why don't you want to tell me?" he asked, placing his fingers under her chin to lift her face to his.

Evelyn drew in a deep breath. "Sharon never liked you," she admitted. "She never trusted you. She always thought you were just stringing me along. Even after we got engaged, she never believed you'd really go through with the marriage."

He seemed to be considering what she'd just said. "Maybe I'm lucky I can't remember much," he said quietly.

She was surprised by his statement. "Why do you say that?" she asked.

He laughed weakly. "Well, I wasn't exactly Prince Charming before the accident, was I?"

"You were human." She stroked his face affectionately. "Sharon just didn't understand you."

"Or maybe she understood me a little too well," Derek suggested.

Evelyn sighed heavily. "Could we talk about something else?" she asked pleadingly. "This is not doing either of us any good."

He surrendered and nodded. "It can wait. What about this Barf Inn? What, exactly, is it?"

She brightened, relieved that the subject had been changed. "Sharon and I opened the restaurant just before I met you. It was a little place then, on the outskirts of the university campus. At first there was no business to speak of. We couldn't get customers even if we'd brought them in at gunpoint. Sharon decided we needed a gimmick. She was the one who came up with the idea Barf Inn. She'd just come back from a vacation in Idaho and brought back some of those barf bags they have on the planes. She thought they would make good carry-out bags. One thing led to another, and we came up with the idea of using double doggy bowls to serve the meals and crackers shaped like dog biscuits—things like that. It was so campy that it caught on. Now it's so in, we could start a chain of Barf Inns on college campuses all over the country and make a fortune."

"Why don't you?" Derek asked, genuinely interested.

She shrugged. "I guess I like the idea of it being a one-of-a-kind thing, of Sharon and me running the whole show ourselves with no one to answer to. Becoming a conglomerate would take all the fun out of it."

He smiled. "I understand that."

"Not that I think we'd ever be as big as Burger King or McDonald's," she went on, "but we had offers, lots of experts who thought we could—"

"It could make you rich."

"Money isn't everything," she said simply.

He was silent for a moment. "God, I wish I could remember, Evelyn," he told her. "I have a feeling I'm missing out on so much by not remembering."

She kissed him. "Maybe," she stated, "I can help you remember."

Chapter Three

"Having an attack of conscience, are we?" Michael wanted to know.

Derek frowned, the mist of the clouds swirling around him. What a place to rendezvous. "I don't know about you, but I sure as h—I sure am," he confessed miserably, gazing downward and feeling more confused than he would have believed possible before his reincarnation.

Michael looked concerned. "She's getting to you, isn't she?"

Derek made a face. "If she weren't, I wouldn't be human."

"You're not," Michael reminded him. "Not anymore, anyway."

"Thanks. I needed to hear that right now."

"Well, you aren't," Michael stated with honesty. "But she does seem to be getting to you, just the same."

"That's a textbook understatement if I've ever heard one."

"Do you want to talk about it?" Michael asked in an attempt to provide the guidance he'd been assigned to give his rookies.

Derek shrugged helplessly. "What is there to talk about?" he wanted to know. "What good would it do?"

"Quite a lot, I should think."

"She's not what I expected," he confided.

"What *did* you expect?" Michael wanted to know.

Derek shrugged again. "I don't know what I expected," he confessed. "A wicked stepmother type, I guess."

Michael laughed. "Aren't you a little old for *Grimm's Fairy Tales?*" he asked, amused.

"Funny."

"But there's more to her than meets the eye," Michael finished.

"Exactly." Derek looked at him, frustrated. "Evelyn is everything Patricia wasn't. She's warm and caring and sensitive—"

"All of the things Patricia was when you married her," Michael reminded him.

"All of the things I *thought* she was," Derek corrected. "Big difference."

"Very," Michael agreed.

"Get to the point, will you?" Derek was growing more irritable by the minute.

"Wasn't Patricia that kind of woman when you married her?" Michael asked.

"Yeah," Derek admitted begrudgingly. "Before ambition got in the way and Dr. Jekyll turned into Mrs. Hyde."

"She must have had some redeeming qualities, or you would not have married her in the first place," Michael reasoned.

"I told you, I thought she had those qualities," Derek snapped crossly.

"Are you such a bad judge of character that she could have fooled you so completely?" Michael asked dubiously. "As I recall, you were quite smitten with her."

"Whose side are you on, anyway?" Derek demanded angrily.

"Yours," Michael assured him. "I'm simply trying to make you see that no one is all good or all bad, and that perhaps you're being too critical of your ex-wife."

"I don't think I'm being hard enough on a woman who walked away from her kids when they needed her most, and who gave them so little of herself," Derek said harshly, refusing to yield where Patricia was concerned.

"You're bitter," Michael said then, without anger or malice, just as a simple statement of fact.

"You're d—of course I'm bitter," Derek admitted, knowing it would do no good to lie to the senior angel.

"Must I remind you that the Boss will not tolerate the pursuit of revenge? If that's your goal, He will yank you from your Earthly existence so fast, it'll make your head spin."

"I'm not interested in revenge," Derek assured him. "I outgrew that long before my—death. I'm only interested in finding the right person to raise my kids."

"Then, let's talk about Evelyn," Michael said promptly. "How does she figure into your current plans?"

"I think Evelyn may be the mother my kids need," Derek answered honestly. "She's everything a mother should be. The other day she told me about how much time she's spent with the kids, how much they mean to her. Realizing it was my kids she was talking about, realizing how much she feels for them, I knew she had to be the one."

"Do you think she's going to be up to motherhood when she loses her fiancé—again?" Michael asked solemnly.

Derek opened his eyes slowly. Today was the big day—he was being released from the hospital. It had been over a week and his physical therapist and doctors were amazed by the speed of his recovery. Jeffrey probably would have done cartwheels at the prospect of going home, but Derek had mixed feelings about it. As anxious as he was to see Patrick and Alexandra— and he planned to swing that as soon as possible—he wasn't at all sure he was ready to get out into the real world and try to *be* Jeffrey Callander.

Can I pull it off? he asked himself. Can I really do it?

Evelyn, who had arrived early to help him dress and pack his suitcase, sensed his ambivalence. She gave him a patient smile. "It must be frightening," she said, as she checked every drawer and shelf, making sure they hadn't forgotten anything.

"What?" he asked, not sure he'd heard her correctly, having been so lost in his own thoughts and doubts about his game plan.

"Reentering the real world." Brushing her long, red hair back off her face, she bent to kiss him lovingly. "You've been here so long, you have to be at least a little nervous about going back to the way things used to be, after all."

"I'd probably be a lot more nervous if I could *remember* how things used to be," he responded.

"It'll be all right," she assured him. "I'll be there with you, helping you every step of the way."

"What if I can't go back?" he asked then.

She paused thoughtfully for a long moment. "In some ways, I suppose that could be for the best," she said quietly.

He looked at her, more confused than ever. "Meaning what?"

She took a deep breath. "Meaning that a near-death experience usually changes a person's life in dramatic ways, and almost always for the better," she explained. "Maybe it's going to do the same for you."

He studied her for a long moment. "I haven't always been Mr. Wonderful in the past, have I?"

Her lips drew into a tight smile. "No, no you haven't," she answered honestly. "But I cared too much to really give up on you."

His own smile was just as strained. "Thank you for not giving up on me, Evelyn," he said softly.

She stopped what she was doing and sat down on the bed beside him. "I couldn't, even if I had wanted to," she said gently. "And there were times, I'll admit, that I *did* want to."

"Maybe we should talk about it," he suggested, wanting to know more.

She shook her head. "Not here, not now," she said. "Right now I just want to enjoy being with the new Jeffrey, to feel grateful to God for giving us another chance."

He took her hands in his and pressed them to his lips. "You won't be sorry you didn't give up on me," he promised her.

But, *I* might be, he was thinking.

"He's changed, Sharon," Evelyn told her sister.

Sharon, a short brunette who had the face—and the mischievous nature—of a pixie, wrinkled her upturned nose disdainfully. "It would have to be a change for the better," she maintained as she went over the day's receipts with the eagle eye of the best CPA. "That one couldn't get any worse."

"He wasn't the monster you thought him to be," Evelyn insisted, defending Jeffrey. "He just wasn't ready to settle down, that's all."

When Sharon looked up from the receipts, her expression was skeptical. "He never will be," she said stubbornly. "And you can probably get odds on that in Vegas."

"Really, Sharon—you haven't seen him since he came out of his coma," Evelyn told her, brushing her hair back over one shoulder as she sipped her iced tea. The cheeseburger on the plate in front of her looked more appealing than it would have if she hadn't eaten all day. "He's like a different man now. I can't explain it. Maybe it's because he had such a close brush with death... I don't know. Whatever the reason, he's reconsidered his own priorities."

"That would do it," Sharon said, nodding emphatically in agreement. "One glimpse of *his* destination in the Hereafter would be enough to turn him into a lifetime choirboy."

"Sharon!"

"Admit it, Ev, that man's put you through forty kinds of agony since the day you met him," Sharon reminded her, as if Evelyn needed to be reminded. It was all too vivid in her memory. "You would have been better off if you'd dumped him after the first date."

"I loved him," Evelyn reminded her, taking a big bite out the cheeseburger.

Sharon made a face. "There's no accounting for taste, big sister."

Evelyn shook her head, wondering if Sharon and Jeffrey would ever bury the hatchet. Only if they can bury it in each other, she told herself. Aloud she said, "I'm thinking of having him stay with us."

"What!" Sharon looked as if she were about to have a stroke.

"Until we find him a suitable live-in nurse," Evelyn explained. "He needs someone who can handle his needs."

"Don't forget the kids," Sharon said. "They won't be pleased and it might hurt your custody issue."

Sharon collected her oversize shoulder bag and two Barf Bags she'd had Cookie, their pseudochef, prepare for herself and her husband, Brian. "Oh, are you coming in tomorrow?"

Evelyn shook her head. "I think I'd better spend the day with Jeffrey."

Sharon waved goodbye as she headed for the door.

After Sharon had gone, Evelyn finished the cheeseburger. She was glad she'd had Cookie make one for her. She knew that she would be too tired to cook for herself by the time she got back to Jeffrey's condo. He would probably be asleep, but she had Cookie fill a Barf Bag for him anyway. He'd never cared for the restaurant's bill of fare, but maybe he wouldn't remember that, either.

Jeffrey *had* changed, but she knew Sharon would have to see it herself to truly believe it. He was so different now, it was as if he were, quite literally, a different person. He looked like Jeffrey, but he acted like someone else.

Evelyn had to admit, if only to herself, that she found it a definite change for the better. While Jeffrey had always been sexy and exciting and intense, the man he was now was also gentle and deeply emotional. All right, so his memory was a little fuzzy, but she could live with that as long as he could. Right now, she felt she could deal with anything.

But then, miracles had a tendency to affect people that way.

"Are you sure?" Evelyn asked.

"I'm sure," Derek said with a nod. "I couldn't eat another bite, I swear."

"You've lost a lot of weight," she reminded him. "You're going to have to eat like a whale to gain it all back."

He acknowledged this with another nod. "Yeah, I know, but not all in one day, please," he begged. "I'll need a few *empty* barf bags if I have to eat another bite."

She hesitated momentarily. "Was it all right?" she asked. "The food, I mean."

"It was better than all right," he assured her. "My compliments to your chef."

Evelyn stared at him for a moment. "You've never liked anything on the Inn's menu before, Jeffrey," she told him.

He looked alarmed at first, as if deeply disturbed by the lack of a memory. "Maybe," he began slowly, "my taste buds have been reawakened, too."

She managed a slight smile. "That's probably it," she agreed.

He reached out and took her hand, giving it an affectionate squeeze. "I know this is unsettling for you, sweetheart," he told her. "But we're going to have a lot of incidents like this. I wish we weren't, but it's unavoidable. It unnerves me, too, but right now, I'm counting my blessings just to be alive, to be able to remember anything at all."

"How much *do* you remember?" she asked then, not really sure she wanted to hear the answer.

His eyes met hers. "Not enough. Not nearly enough."

Finding a live-in nurse for Jeffrey proved easier than Evelyn expected. One call to the local Visiting Nurses office had produced a middle-aged, pleasant, energetic woman named Mary O'Malley with whom she hit it off immediately. This, she decided, was someone she could trust to care for Jeffrey in her absence. Mary reminded Evelyn of her own mother.

The only objections came from Jeffrey himself.

"I don't need a baby-sitter," he argued.

"I agree," Evelyn responded. "But you *do* need a nurse."

"For what?"

"Come on, Jeffrey. You know what the doctors said. You could come home *only* if you had round-the-clock care," she reminded him.

"You're here."

"But I'm not here all the time."

"You could be."

"No, I couldn't," she told him. "I do have other responsibilities, you know. The restaurant, the children..."

"You and the kids could move in with me," he suggested.

"No, we couldn't."

"Why not?"

"Do you even have to ask?"

He hesitated, a flicker of recognition in his eyes. "I'm sorry," he told her. "I didn't realize we hadn't been—uh, intimate before the accident."

Evelyn tried not to laugh. "It's not that," she said. "It's the children."

"What about them?"

"I don't think moving them in with you would be such a good idea, that's all."

"Why not?"

"You really *don't* remember, do you?"

"Remember what?"

"You weren't exactly good with kids."

"They didn't like me?"

She hesitated. "You didn't like them."

He frowned. "Did I mistreat them?" he wanted to know.

"No," Evelyn began carefully, "you just weren't very good with them. You didn't like being around them. I thought you'd adjust but you stayed firm."

"I don't remember it, but I promise you, it's going to change," he said. "I'll work on it."

"I'd appreciate it." She'd have to see it to believe it.

He'd finally given in on the matter of a live-in nurse, but made it clear he wasn't crazy about the idea. "I just have one question," he told her as she was leaving.

"Yes?"

"*Were* we intimate before the accident?"

She smiled slyly. "I'll never tell."

It was going to be one of those nights.

Evelyn had hoped that, with the passing of time, the children would show signs that they were beginning to accept the loss of their father, but so far, it didn't seem to be happening as the so-called experts had told her it would. There were all-too-frequent nights that they cried themselves to sleep no matter what she said or did, longing for the man who had simply disappeared from their lives one day without warning.

With Patrick fighting back tears and Alexandra hanging on to her for dear life as if she might disappear, too, at any moment, Evelyn decided she had to do something, give them something positive to hold on to. Finally, after much thought and even more desperation, it came to her. Carrying Alexandra in one arm, she took Patrick's hand and brought them over to the window, where they could have an unobstructed view of the night sky. "Remember what I told you about your father always being with you, always looking down from the heavens to watch over you?" she asked.

"Y-y-yes," Patrick said chokingly.

"Look up there," she said, pointing skyward.

"At the sky?"

"At the *stars.*"

He nodded, but it was clear neither of them realized what she was doing yet.

"Whenever someone dies, when they go to Heaven to be with God, a new star appears in the sky," she explained. "The new star is where that person lives, where he is all the time. That's so he has a good spot from which to look down on his loved ones."

"You mean Daddy's up there watching us?" Patrick asked.

Evelyn smiled. "He sure is."

"I see him!" Alexandra cried excitedly. "Over there...see?"

"I see him, too!" Patrick shouted. "That real bright one."

"By golly, you must be right," Evelyn said, hugging them both. "It is the brightest one out tonight."

She smiled to herself as she left them to admire Daddy's star for a while. It wasn't much, but it was a start. We'll see, she told herself.

This time, when she put them to bed, they didn't cry. "I can see Daddy from here," Alexandra told her as she tucked the child in.

"Of course you can," Evelyn said, "and as long as you can, you'll always know you're safe, that he's looking out for you."

The child smiled up at her. "I wish you were my mommy."

Evelyn held her tightly for a long moment. "I wish it, too, baby," she told her.

She had never meant anything more in her life.

Chapter Four

"If you're satisfied, then there's really no need to stick around, is there?" Michael reasoned.

"Don't rush it," Derek responded irritably. "I have nearly fifty days left. I'd like to take all of them, if you don't mind."

"I *do* mind," Michael told him. "The longer you stay on Earth, the more likely you are to land yourself in some kind of trouble."

"What makes you so sure I'll end up in trouble?" Derek asked.

"Your track record speaks for itself," Michael reminded him. "Your basic nature doesn't really change all that much when you enter the Hereafter."

"Thanks for the vote of confidence," Derek grumbled.

"I'm required to be honest," Michael said. "It's part of the job description."

"Let's make it interesting, then," Derek said promptly. "You say I'll screw up. I say I won't. I propose a little wager."

Michael's eyebrows shot upward. "A bet?" he asked. "Are you suggesting a *bet?*"

"Well, yes." Derek suddenly had the uncomfortable feeling he'd screwed up again—in a major way.

Michael reprimanded him. "This is exactly the sort of thing I've been concerned about. We are not permitted to gamble. You already know that."

"You can't blame me for trying," Derek grumbled.

"Yes, I can," Michael disagreed. "And more important, the Boss can. You're not scoring any brownie points here, Derek."

"Look, Michael," Derek began, suddenly humble. "All I want is to spend a little time with my kids before I have to come back—is that too much to ask?"

Michael frowned. "You *do* realize that the more time you spend with them, the harder it will be to leave them when your time is finally up—" he began.

Derek gave a reluctant nod. "I know, but any time is better than no time at all."

"Is it?" Michael asked dubiously.

"Yes, it is," Derek insisted. "I haven't even seen the kids yet. Evelyn hasn't been wildly enthusiastic about the idea of bringing them for a visit."

"Well, you have to remember that Jeffrey Callander hasn't exactly been thrilled at the prospect of fatherhood, instant or otherwise," Michael reminded him.

"That's the hard part, having to remember that I'm Jeffrey Callander, not Derek Wolfe," Derek lamented. "Remembering he's been a louse with his fiancée and doesn't like kids. This guy would have been perfect for Patricia.''

''Difficult, isn't it?'' Michael asked. ''Having to assume the identity of someone you don't like very much, I mean.''

''It's a pain in the—'' Derek caught himself. ''It's no walk in the park, that's for sure.''

''Would you really want to have to do it for sixty days?'' Michael was skeptical.

Derek opened his mouth to respond, then stopped himself. ''Nice try, Mike.'' He chuckled, only half amused.

''I haven't a clue as to what you're talking about,'' Michael sniffed. ''And don't call me Mike!''

''You're playing shrink with me, but it's not going to work,'' Derek told him.

''Shrink?'' Michael looked genuinely perplexed.

''Trying to make me see what a bummer it would be to have to live in old Jeffrey's skin for two whole months,'' Derek said. ''Trying to show me how much better off I'd be if I'd just throw in the towel and come back.''

''I think this is a mistake. I've already said that,'' Michael said evenly. ''I don't need to psyche you, nor would I try.''

''Sure.'' Derek sucked in his breath, knowing it would do no good to debate the issue with Michael. The bad thing about angels was that they were never wrong. ''I'd better get back,'' he said aloud. ''It's almost morning down there.''

''C'mon guys, breakfast is ready!'' Evelyn called out.

"Coming!" A few moments later, Patrick and Alexandra bounded down the stairs and raced past Evelyn, into the kitchen.

Sundays were their days together. Evelyn spent most of the day, if not all of it, with the children, starting with breakfast. Sunday breakfasts were special because everyone had what they wanted, even if that meant Evelyn had to cook three completely different meals. Today, Patrick had requested blueberry pancakes, while Alexandra wanted eggs. Evelyn was having waffles with peach topping. She squeezed fresh orange juice for all of them and made biscuits, which she served with butter and honey.

"What're we going to do today?" Patrick asked when everyone was seated at the table.

"Let's go to the zoo!" Alexandra chirped.

"We went to the zoo last week," Patrick protested. "Let's go to the video arcade."

"I hate the arcade," Alexandra objected. "All the big kids won't let me play. Let's go to the movies. Patrick can play video games at the movies."

"Actually," Evelyn began, buttering herself a biscuit. "I was thinking maybe we'd all go see Jeffrey today. He's home from the hospital now, you know."

Patrick made a face. "I don't want to go to Jeff's," he complained. "He's a jerkface."

"Patrick!"

"It's the truth," he insisted stubbornly. "He doesn't like us, Alexandra and me. He doesn't like kids at all. He wouldn't *want* us coming to visit."

"That's not true," Evelyn said.

"Yes, it is," he argued. "He's just like our mother."

Evelyn didn't know what to say, how to respond to that. She knew the kids' mother had abandoned them when they were young, had left them with their father at a time when they'd needed her most while she'd gone off to God only knew where to pursue her own ambitions. Not that Evelyn faulted any woman for having her own needs and ambitions. Far from it. But she had no empathy for any woman who would turn her back on her own children for any reason.

"Jeffrey's changed," Evelyn said finally. "He's not like he used to be."

"They gave him 'nice' shots in the hospital?" Alexandra wanted to know.

Evelyn tried not to laugh. "Something like that, yes."

"He likes kids now?"

Evelyn wasn't sure about that, but she was optimistic. "I think so, yes—but I think he needs to see you, spend time with you."

Patrick gave a reluctant sigh. "I guess we *could* go see him. For a little while," he grumbled.

Evelyn leaned across the table to kiss his forehead. "Thank you."

"I brought the children with me," Evelyn told Derek. "I hope you don't mind."

"Not at all." He was beginning to think she'd never bring them around. "Where are they?"

"Downstairs. I figured I'd better make sure you were up to it before I sprung them on you."

"Bring them up," he urged. "I'd love to see them."

Evelyn hesitated. The look on her face said, is this really *Jeffrey* saying this? It wasn't, of course, but if he told her the truth, she'd really think he'd lost it.

"Sure," she responded uneasily. "I'll be right back."

She left the room, returning a few minutes later with the children. They eyed him warily, hanging back, clinging to Evelyn. They're behaving as if she's taking them to the dentist, he thought, angry with Jeffrey for being such a louse and making them afraid of him. What was a decent woman like Evelyn doing with a jerk like Jeffrey Callander, anyway?

"C'mon in, kids," he urged.

They stepped forward hesitantly. "Hello, Jeffrey," Patrick greeted him, his ambivalence still very much in evidence.

"Hi, guy." He smiled warmly, trying to think of a way to break the ice. "Lexi, cat got your tongue?"

The confused look on Alexandra's face told him he'd goofed. Only Derek called her Lexi—and that was something he used to say to her when she was uncharacteristically quiet.

"My daddy used to say that to me," Alexandra told him, echoing his own memories.

"Did he, now?" He smiled. "I hope you don't mind me saying it, then."

She frowned. "I guess not."

Patrick tugged at Evelyn's sleeve. "What's with him?" the boy wanted to know. "He's not acting like him."

"He was in a bad accident," Evelyn tried to explain. "He doesn't remember a lot of things. I told you that before we came over."

"He doesn't remember the bad stuff, then?"

"Not much."

"He likes us now?" This was Alexandra.

"You bet I do," Derek responded. "And I want to make it up to you—to both of you—for not being a very nice guy before."

"Lighten up, Derek." This was Michael's voice, speaking to him from wherever. *"You're trying too hard. Beware of overkill."*

"Overkill?"

"Overkill. You sound phony. Take it slow."

"I'll try. But it's not easy. I'm only human."

"Not anymore."

"Thanks. I needed that."

"Yes, I believe you did."

"Get to the point, will you?"

"I thought I already had."

"Right. Don't overdo it."

"Not a good idea, Derek. This is a very perceptive woman, and you've already aroused her suspicions."

"You think so?"

"Don't you?"

He looked at Evelyn, who definitely looked more than a little curious. *"You may be right, Mike."*

"I told you—"

"I know, I know. Michael."

"Thank you."

"You're welcome. Now, will you please go away?"

"Gladly. But I'll be back."

"That's what I'm afraid of."

"I'll pretend I didn't hear that."

"Yeah."

"Jeffrey?"

Evelyn's voice cut through his thoughts. His head jerked up. "I'm sorry," he quickly apologized. "I still fade out sometimes."

Evelyn nodded, and he could tell she'd assumed it was an aftereffect from the accident. "Don't worry about it," she said reassuringly. "It's to be expected."

"Yeah, I guess." He motioned to the children again. "C'mon over. I don't bite."

"You used to," Alexandra told him.

Patrick gave her a hard poke with his elbow. "She didn't mean that," he said quickly.

"Yes, I did."

"Shut up, Alex!"

Derek frowned. He must have been worse than a louse, he thought. The kids are scared to death of him—me. This is as confusing as—it's confusing. "Well, that's all going to change," he said aloud. "I don't want you to be afraid of me anymore. I want us to be friends. Good friends."

Finally, Patrick climbed up on the bed, followed by a still somewhat reluctant Alexandra.

"You don't have to be so careful." Derek chuckled. "I'm not in any pain. You won't hurt me."

But he knew the truth, that the kids were undoubtedly always cautious around Jeffrey Callander. If this guy had lived, if he'd married Evelyn, he—Derek—would not have wanted her to have permanent custody of the kids. This guy was definitely *not* cut out to be a father.

He wasn't cut out to be a husband, either, for that matter.

What could Evelyn possibly have seen in him?

Probably the same thing I saw in Patricia, he decided. Too much that wasn't for real and too little of what was.

"We're going to start doing things together, just as soon as the doctors give me the okay," he promised. "You guys ever been to a wrestling match?"

Both children brightened immediately. "Our daddy used to take us all the time," said Patrick.

"Great. Who are your favorite wrestlers?" he wanted to know.

"Sonny Simms!" they both responded without hesitation.

"Sonny Simms?" He grinned. "Oh, yeah—big guy in black leather, rides a motorcycle? Looks like Fu Manchu?"

Patrick made a face. "Fu—who?" he asked.

"A guy with a long mustache," Derek offered in explanation.

"That's Sonny," Patrick said, nodding.

"We like Sonny. He's tough," Alexandra chirped.

"Sonny's mean," Patrick agreed.

"Then it's settled," Derek said promptly. "As soon as I'm back on my feet, we're going to the wrestling matches. I'll get tickets for Sonny Simms's next appearance here."

"All right!"

"Right now, I think Jeffrey needs to get some rest," Evelyn interrupted. "Why don't you go downstairs and watch TV? I'll be down in a little while."

"Awww—"

"Scoot," she ordered.

Pouting, the children did as they were told. Evelyn let them out of the room, then closed the door. When she turned back to Derek, she had an odd look on her face.

"What's wrong?" he asked.

"You've always hated wrestling."

"I didn't blow it. She believed it was just one more change resulting from the accident," Derek insisted.

"How long do you think you can go on using that lame excuse?" Michael wanted to know.

"Lame excuse? How can you call it a lame excuse? The poor guy was in a serious accident," he said. "He was in a coma. It's bound to have had a major effect on him—"

"Give me a break!" Michael cut him off. "Poor guy? Not twenty minutes ago you thought he was a no-good jerkface!"

"Regardless of what I think of him, the guy went through a major trauma," Derek argued. "It's conceivable that he could be drastically changed by it."

"Conceivable, yes," Michael conceded. "Likely, no."

"So what are you trying to tell me in your not-so-subtle way?" Derek asked.

"That should be crystal clear," Michael sniffed. "I'm telling you to get off your lazy duff and bone up on Jeffrey Callander. Stop relying on amnesia to get you by."

"And just how am I supposed to 'bone up' on him?" Derek asked.

"Just imagine how he felt and try to get people to talk about him more. Go through old photo albums and listen for a change."

He's not the louse I thought he was, Derek decided as he put down the diaries, photo albums and newspaper clippings on Jeffrey's family Evelyn had brought in to jog his memory. Actually, we have quite a lot in common.

They'd both been burned—in different ways, but with very similar results. They were both afraid to love, to give of themselves emotionally, yet both of them *had* loved quite deeply. Both of them still had strong emotional ties among the living.

Both of them had a stake in the outcome of Derek's stay on Earth.

He opened his eyes as Evelyn came into the room, smiling warmly at the sight of her. "What a way to start the day," he said.

She smiled. "Glad to see me, are you?" Holding his breakfast tray with both hands, she bumped the door with her hip to push it all the way open.

"I'm always glad to see you," he insisted.

She laughed. "I don't know what happened to you while you were out," she started, "but I think I like the change."

He smiled. "I'm glad."

"I have to admit that I'm surprised by the way you've changed toward the children," she said, positioning the tray across his lap. "Before the accident, you had very little to do with them."

He paused. "It wasn't that I didn't like them," he said finally. "I was afraid to get too attached to them."

She looked dubious. "Why?"

"C'mon, Evelyn—you've got them on a temporary basis," he reminded her. "You've said yourself that nobody's been too optimistic about your chances of getting permanent custody."

She frowned. "I haven't given up."

"I know you haven't," he said gently. "I just couldn't let myself get too close to them, knowing they could be taken away at any time."

"What changed your mind?" she wanted to know.

He shook his head sadly. "You can't come as close to death as I did without being changed by it, without rethinking your priorities," he told her.

"Who hurt you?" Evelyn asked then. "Who made you so afraid to love?"

"It's a long story," he answered evasively.

"I've got the time."

He shook his head again. "Maybe some other time."

She rolled her eyes upward in exasperation. "I hate it when you do that," she said with a heavy sigh.

"Do what?"

"Shut me out like that."

"I wasn't shutting you out—" he began.

"You've always shut me out," she declared. "Some things haven't changed at all."

"I've never meant to shut you out," he insisted.

"But you *have*," she told him. "Every time we have a conversation like this, and you really start to open up to me, it's like an alarm goes off in your head and an invisible wall goes up, keeping me at bay. It's another reason why we almost broke up."

Derek's mind was racing, trying to determine what Jeffrey would do, what he would say. That's easy, he thought. Jeffrey would clam up. Jeffrey would shut her out, just as she says he has. He wouldn't intend to, he wouldn't want to, but he'd do it.

Aloud he said, "Give it time. I'm trying, Ev, but it's hard to break the habits of a lifetime."

She studied him for a moment, then nodded. "It's not easy, Jeff," she told him.

"I know. And I'm sorry."

"I love you, Jeff."

He hesitated. "Me, too." Would Jeffrey have told her he loved her? Would he have said the words? He doubted it.

Play it cool, he told himself. Don't lose sight of why you're here. Don't forget it's just a temporary thing.

Don't make promises you won't be able to keep.

It was hard not to comfort her, not to try to explain her fiancé's behavior to her, but he knew he couldn't.

"You never say it," she observed.

"Say what?"

"You never tell me you love me."

"I just did."

"No, you didn't," she disagreed. "I said, 'I love you,' and you said, 'Me, too.'"

"That's not the same thing?" he asked, already knowing the answer.

She shook her head. "No, it isn't. You never really say the words," she pointed out. "You wait for me to say it, then you say 'me, too' or 'ditto' or something like that. You never say 'I love you, Evelyn,' or 'I love you, too.' Never."

"A lot of men have that problem," he reminded her.

"And some of you don't even try to correct it," she said.

"If you'll just—"

"I know—give it time." Evelyn sighed. "How much time do you really need?"

Impulsively, he leaned forward and kissed her forehead. "I've never meant to hurt you, Evelyn," he told her.

He was sure Jeffrey hadn't, either. But he had anyway.

Chapter Five

"He's like a completely different man," Evelyn told her sister.

Sharon gave her a skeptical look. "You couldn't get that lucky."

Evelyn stopped what she was doing and turned to look at her. "You could at least give him a chance," she said.

"I've given him a lot of chances, Ev—more chances than he's deserved," Sharon reminded her. "He talks a good game, but he never delivers."

"This time he really has changed," Evelyn insisted. "You should see him with the children. Would you believe he's promised to take them to a wrestling match?"

"No, I wouldn't believe." Sharon ducked under the counter to check their supply of Barf Bags. "What's he want?"

"Really, Sharon—"

"I'm serious. He must want something." Sharon checked the cash drawer.

"Not this time," Evelyn said confidently. "This time he really has changed."

"Then we'd better prepare ourselves 'cause Judgment Day must surely be just around the corner." Sharon went on to check all the soda machines and coffeemakers to verify that they were all filled and operating.

"You should see him with the kids," Evelyn said then.

Sharon turned to face her again. "What about you?" she asked. "How is he with *you* now?"

"Different—for the most part."

"For the most part?"

"Sometimes—though not very often—he sounds like the old Jeffrey," Evelyn admitted.

"Sounds like him—how?" Sharon asked.

"He's still afraid to let himself care too much," Evelyn said quietly. "He won't talk about it, but I know he's been badly hurt at some point in his life by someone he really cared about."

"Like who?"

"I wish I knew." Evelyn frowned. "That's the one part of his life he's never been willing to share with me."

"One of many, I'll bet."

"Why do you dislike him so much?" Evelyn asked then. "I'm the one who's had to live with him—so to speak."

"Exactly—and if I didn't care about you, I wouldn't say a word," Sharon told her. "But I *do* care. You're my favorite sister."

"I'm your only sister," Evelyn pointed out.

"Don't change the subject," Sharon grumbled. "You've changed since you got involved with him. A lot."

"How do you figure?"

"You were a different person when you first got involved with him, Ev," Sharon remembered. "You used to be fun. You used to have a sense of humor. You used to enjoy things, enjoy life. Now you're like an old woman."

"Thanks a lot." The comment hurt a lot more than Evelyn was willing to let on.

"I'm sorry," Sharon said quietly, "but it's true. It's like being involved with him has aged you."

Evelyn drew in a deep breath. "Look, I've got to leave. Patrick has a doctor's appointment. Can you manage here without me?" she asked.

"Sure, but—"

Evelyn cut her off. "We'll finish this conversation later."

"Evelyn—"

But she was already out the door.

Evelyn didn't want to admit it, even to herself, but Sharon was right.

Her troubled relationship with Jeffrey had changed her. As wonderful as it had been in the beginning, the problems had eventually taken their toll on her. She knew she hadn't been much fun to be around, especially since Jeffrey's accident. She knew most of her friends agreed with Sharon, that they thought Jeffrey was bad for her, that he'd made a mess of her life. There were times she'd seriously considered getting out of the relationship. Finally she had broken the engagement.

She'd believed he'd never change, but he had.

She'd believed it wouldn't get any better, but...

It *is* getting better.

She really believed that. He was so different now, since he came out of the coma. He was more caring, more giving.

To an extent.

There was still something there, something that made him hold back. If only she knew what that something was. She'd know what she was up against. She'd know how to deal with it.

Maybe.

As it was, she was shooting in the dark.

He was asleep when she entered the room. He slept a lot. Sometimes she worried that he slept too much, and she considered speaking to his doctor about it. Other times, she told herself he'd been through so much physically, he was bound to do a lot of sleeping until he'd fully regained his strength.

He opened his eyes as if he'd sensed her presence. "Hi, lady," he said, smiling.

"Hi yourself."

"How do you do it?"

She gave him a quizzical look. "How do I do what?"

"Everything at once." He pulled himself into an upright position. "How do you run a restaurant, take care of two children *and* play Florence Nightingale?"

"Well, for one thing, I don't have to run the restaurant by myself," she said, seating herself on the corner of the bed. "Sharon spends more time there than I do."

"Sharon?"

"My sister."

"Ah, yes."

"You still don't remember her, do you?" Evelyn asked.

"Not really," he admitted, somewhat embarrassed.

"I can't wait to get the two of you together," she said, amused by the possibilities that played in her mind.

He grinned. "So—you do have a mischievous side."

It bothered her that he obviously had no memory of that side of her personality, especially after the comment Sharon had made. Aloud she said, "According to my sister, I used to."

His smile vanished. "Did I say something wrong?" he wanted to know.

"No, why?"

"You seemed—offended."

She hesitated. "My sister tells me I'm no fun anymore," she admitted, "so..."

"So, when I said that, I really stuck my foot in my mouth," he finished.

"Well, yes."

"I'm sorry."

"Don't be. I'm starting to realize that Sharon just might be right," she said.

"No, she's not."

She knew what he was trying to do, and she loved him for it. But she didn't believe it for a minute.

As if sensing what she was feeling, he abruptly changed the subject. "What about the kids?"

She wasn't sure what he meant. "What about them?"

"They must be a handful."

She gave a little laugh. "That they are," she admitted.

"Do you ever have any regrets?" he asked hesitantly.

"Regrets? About having the kids?" She was genuinely surprised by the question. "Never!"

"You're sure?"

"Absolutely," she insisted. "Why do you even ask?"

"I don't know," he began. "It just seems like you've taken on an incredible amount of responsibility at once. Not just the kids—everything. I just wondered if the enormity of the burden ever got to you."

She gave him a weary smile. "There are times I'm so exhausted, I can barely hold my head up," she confessed. "Some days I think only an act of God will get me out of bed. There are times I think I'd be better off if I sold my interest in the restaurant and got a job working for someone else, if that makes any sense at all. There are days I'm glad there's a nurse here most of the time. But, no matter how rough it gets sometimes, I've never regretted having taken those children."

His eyes met hers. "I think you really mean that."

"I've never meant anything more in my life."

"She's incredible—absolutely incredible," Derek told Michael.

"Don't get too attached to her," Michael cautioned.

"Don't be ridiculous!" Derek snorted. "I was referring to her commitment to the kids—and *only* her commitment to the kids."

"You're sure about that, are you?" Michael asked dubiously.

"Yes, I *am*," he insisted. "She's totally devoted to Patrick and Alexandra—the way Patricia should have been, but never was."

"Patricia again."

"Evelyn adores the kids, and they're crazy about her, too," Derek went on, ignoring Michael's observation about his still-bitter feelings toward his ex-wife.

"It sounds to me as if you've developed some fairly strong, positive feelings of your own for the lady," Michael said.

"Nonsense! The only feelings I have for Evelyn concern her relationship with my kids!" Derek insisted.

"I think this is what you would like to believe," Michael responded, unconvinced.

"Hogwash!"

"So when can I start behaving like a normal human being again?" Derek asked the doctor.

The older man completed his physical examination of his patient and gave him a satisfied smile. "I don't see why you can't begin to rejoin the human race now," he answered. "Provided, of course, you use a little common sense."

"Common sense?"

"I think you know what I'm talking about," the doctor said. "Start slow. Do a little at a time. Don't try to do more than you're physically up to."

"In other words—"

"In other words, don't overdo it," the doctor summarized.

"Don't worry about that," Derek said cheerfully. "I'm so glad to be back among the living, there's no way I'm going to do anything to risk it."

"That's good to hear." The doctor put away his stethoscope and made some notes in Jeffrey Callander's file. "Should I take this to mean that you're giving up skydiving, Formula One racing and polo?"

"Absolutely."

"For now, anyway."

"For good." It would be easier, Derek decided, than trying to explain to the people who knew Jeffrey best why he suddenly didn't know how to do any of those things.

"I'm going to have to see that to believe it," the doctor said with a chuckle. "I've been your physician for almost twenty years now, and I've patched you up after more accidents than I can count—but no matter what, you never gave it up."

"I never came that close to death before," Derek pointed out.

"True."

"Take my word for it, Doc. Jeffrey Callander has retired from the danger circuit."

"So, what did Dr. Ellis have to say?" Evelyn asked on the way home.

"He gave me a clean bill of health."

"Meaning what exactly?" Evelyn wanted to know.

"Meaning just what I said. He gave me a clean bill of health." He grinned. "I'm a fully functional human being again."

She eyed him suspiciously from the corner of one eye as she negotiated the unusually heavy traffic. "Fully functional?" she asked dubiously.

"Fully functional," he repeated for emphasis.

"So I guess that means you can pretty much do whatever you want now, right?"

"Pretty much, yeah."

"Who are you trying to kid, Jeff?" She kept her eyes on the road out of necessity, so she didn't see the look of surprise on his face.

"I beg your pardon?"

"You heard me. Who are you trying to kid?" she asked again. "You were in a serious accident. You were in a coma. You almost died, Jeffrey. No doctor in his right mind would let you become 'fully functional' again this soon."

He was silent for a moment. "Okay, so he didn't exactly say I was up to a hundred percent just yet," Derek confessed. "But he did say I could stop playing the bedridden invalid."

"What, precisely, *did* he say?"

"He said I could start doing normal things again," Derek answered. "I could pretty much do what I wanted as long as I don't get into anything too stressful physically and don't overdo it."

"Why didn't you tell me that in the first place?" she asked.

"Well," he began carefully, "I didn't want you to worry. I have something special planned for my first outing."

"Really?" Evelyn envisioned a romantic candlelight dinner at their favorite restaurant overlooking Puget Sound. "Just what did you have in mind?"

"I'm taking the kids to the wrestling match."

Evelyn made a concerted effort not to let her disappointment show, but she *was* deeply disappointed.

From the moment Jeffrey came out of the coma, from the day the doctors told her he was going to recover, she'd always believed that his return to the world of the living would be marked by a very private, romantic celebration, with just the two of them.

Never once did she imagine he'd want to spend his first night out with the kids at, of all things, a wrestling match.

Maybe he'd changed more than she wanted him to.

Shame on you, Evelyn Sloan, she scolded herself. It sounds like you're jealous of your own children.

My own children.

I wish.

Will it ever happen?

No one who counted in such matters seemed to think it was likely. In fact, she'd been told, more than once, that the odds were against it.

They said if she were married, it would make a difference.

How archaic, she thought resentfully.

If anyone had told her, even a year ago, that she'd even consider a marriage of convenience, for the sake of the children, she would have told them there were nuts. But now . . . now she was willing to consider just about anything that might help her gain permanent custody of Patrick and Alexandra.

It's ironic, she thought dismally. Jeffrey's finally accepted the kids, but he's no closer to making a real commitment to our relationship than he's ever been.

In spite of the change in him.

"I can't wait to tell Bobby Meeks about this," Patrick said, referring to another boy in Evelyn's neighborhood, as Derek preceded them through the crowded, noisy arena to the long, cavelike corridor that led to the wrestlers' dressing rooms. "He's gonna be green when he finds out I actually met Sonny Simms!"

Derek said a silent thank-you to the real Jeffrey Callander, whose family's wealth and position in the city meant there were connections available that had enabled him to arrange a prematch visit with the champ.

As they approached Sonny Simms's dressing room, a beautiful, petite blonde woman came storming out, yelling at the top of her lungs. Derek didn't have to ask to know that the woman was the champ's wife, actress Heather Simms. According to tabloids such as the *International Intruder,* Sonny Simms had gone more rounds with Heather than he had with his opponents.

But then, who could believe the tabloids? Derek thought, amused. They even published stories about people who had claimed to have seen angels on Earth!

Given Heather's unceremonious departure from the dressing room, Derek wondered what kind of mood the champ was in. Probably not in the mood for visitors, he thought worriedly.

"Aren't we going in?" Patrick asked, interrupting his thoughts.

"What? Oh sure," Derek assured him, tapping on the large door gingerly.

"Yeah, whaddya want?" It was more of a growl than a voice, making Derek think of a mean old bear that had been prematurely roused from its hibernation.

"A couple of young fans to see you, Mr. Simms."

The voice coming from the other side of the door was suddenly, unexpectedly warm. "In that case, come on in," he responded.

Derek opened the door, ushering Patrick and Alexandra inside. The heavyweight wrestling champion, Sonny Simms, stood in the center of the room, a mountain of a man, all hard muscle and exaggerated Fu Manchu mustache, wearing black trunks and a muscle shirt. The championship belt was strapped around his waist.

He broke into a huge grin. "Hi, kids," he boomed.

"Hi, Champ!" Patrick responded enthusiastically.

Alexandra hung back a little, not saying anything.

Sonny Simms knelt on the floor in front of her. "You don't have to be afraid, princess," he told her. "I like kids. It's everybody else I can't stand."

Alexandra giggled.

Derek extended his hand and introduced himself. "Jeffrey Callander, Mr. Simms."

"Oh, yeah, you talked to Billy Ray," Sonny remembered as they shook hands.

"Billy Ray?" Alexandra asked. "Billy Ray Cyrus?"

"No, Lexi." Derek chuckled. "Another Billy Ray. A different one."

Sonny looked surprised. "Ain't she a little young to be into Billy Ray Cyrus?"

Derek shrugged. "When *do* girls start having those feelings?" he asked.

"Wouldn't know." Sonny stood up. "I think my Heather Anne must've started while she was still in diapers."

Derek was silent, knowing better than to comment on *that*.

He had the distinct feeling that he was going to be going a few rounds himself over this outing—with Michael, and with Evelyn.

"You must have worn them out," Evelyn said as she came down the stairs. "They went to sleep almost the moment their heads hit the pillows."

Derek laughed. "Actually, they wore me out," he confessed. "It's hard to imagine anyone having that much energy."

"It's not hard for me," she assured him. "I've been witness to it for the past six months. They've completely exhausted me more than once."

"I couldn't believe it," he told her. "They jumped up and down in their seats and yelled and shouted and cheered. I lost track of how many sodas were spilled, how many boxes of popcorn ended up on the floor. I bought them hot dogs, but I don't think either of them took more than a bite or two."

"When you take them anywhere like that, it's usually better to take them out to eat first." Evelyn sat next to him on the couch. "They get too excited to eat."

He was silent for a moment. "I really haven't spent much time with them, have I?" he asked.

Evelyn frowned. "Until now, you haven't spent *any* time with them," she told him.

"Well, that's going to change," he promised her.

She didn't respond right away. She was pleased that he wanted to spend more time with Patrick and Alexandra, but she still wasn't sure where that left her. What did he want for them? What kind of future, if any, did he want with her?

She finally decided to ask him about it. "What about us, Jeffrey?"

He looked surprised—or perhaps unnerved—by her question. "What *about* us?"

"What's going to happen with us?" she asked. "We've been coasting for a long time now."

"Coasting?"

She nodded. "Even before your accident, we've been in relationship limbo," she told him. "We'd been seeing each other for a long time. We were engaged. Yet our relationship wasn't moving forward." She wasn't sure she should tell him she'd broken their engagement. At least not yet, not until he'd fully recovered.

He avoided her eyes. "I wish I could remember these things you're telling me," he said quietly.

"So do I." She sighed heavily. "At the time of your accident, I had already begun to wonder whether or not we had a future together."

He gave her a quizzical look. "We *were* engaged," he pointed out. "Why would you have doubts—"

"I had doubts because we didn't seem to be going any further than that." Evelyn paused. "I hope I don't sound like a desperate woman, because I'm really not. I'm just frustrated. I need to know where we're going, if anywhere."

"I wish I had the answers you need," he said, obviously at a loss.

"Do you love me, Jeffrey?" she asked then.

He looked startled. "What kind of question is that?"

"An honest one, I think."

"We *are* engaged, Evelyn," he reminded her. "I don't think I would have asked you to marry me if I didn't."

"You don't *think*—"

"I really don't remember a lot about our life as a couple—or much of anything else, for that matter—prior to the accident. You know that," he said. "I want our life to be what it was. Better, if possible. But I'm going to need some time. I'm going to need you to be patient. Can you give me that?"

"Jeffrey, I'd give you anything you needed if I believed there was any hope at all for us," she told him.

He stood up. "Look, I'm beat," he said wearily. "I think we ought to sleep on this for now." He bent to kiss her cheek. "We'll talk later, okay?"

It wasn't until after he was gone that she realized he never had said he loved her.

Maybe I went too far, Evelyn thought worriedly.

She lay awake that night, thinking about it. He *had* been right. It *was* going to take time for them to establish a normal relationship again—let alone a good one—after what he'd been through. He had so little memory of the past—their past. It was bound to take time.

What troubled her most wasn't what they were going through now, but what they'd been going through *before* the accident. If their relationship had been on a solid footing before the accident, she wouldn't feel so ambivalent now. She was less sure of Jeffrey now than she had been that morning he went diving in Puget Sound.

In the beginning, at the start of their relationship, he'd been so warm, so passionate—such an ardent

suitor. He'd made her feel like the most desirable
woman on Earth. In retrospect, however, it seemed to
Evelyn that the closer they became emotionally, the
more ambivalent Jeffrey had become, and the more
he'd tried to withdraw from her, from the relationship.

She'd always felt that there was something in Jeffrey's past that made him fear commitment, but
whatever it was, he refused to talk about it. She'd been
left to speculate, and she speculated often. It had to be
a woman. She was sure it must have been a former
lover. That was the only possibility that made any
sense. He'd been involved with someone—and he
must have loved her very deeply, Evelyn concluded, to
have been so strongly affected by her betrayal, whatever it was.

Evelyn wondered if he could have simply lost interest in *her*. She hadn't been able to forget what Sharon
had said that day at the restaurant. She really had
changed. She wasn't the same woman she'd been when
she first became involved with Jeffrey. She knew she
hadn't been much fun to be around lately.

Maybe, she thought, it was time for that to change.

"I feel like a heel," Derek told Michael.

"You're doing what you have to do," Michael reminded him. "This is only a temporary arrangement.
To encourage her, to make promises you haven't a
prayer of keeping, would be cruel."

"Tell me about it."

"I just did."

"Funny as a crutch, Michael."

"Really?" the senior angel sniffed. "I wasn't trying to be amusing."

"I'd hate to see what would happen if you *did* try, then," Derek grumbled.

"What about the children?"

Derek's frown changed abruptly to a smile. "Ah, the kids are great. It feels so good to be able to spend time with them," he admitted. "I've missed that more than anything."

"I can't believe you took them to a wrestling match," Michael said then.

Derek let out an exaggerated groan. "You sound like my mother," he told the senior angel.

Michael ignored the insult. "I would think they'd be too young for that sort of thing," he stated flatly.

"Nah, kids get into sports at a much earlier age than they did when you and I were growing up," Derek said.

"Sports!" Michael snorted. "Everyone knows wrestling is more theater than sport."

"Not everyone," Derek said with a grin.

"And while we're on the subject," Michael went on, "do you consider the likes of Sonny Simms a positive role model for your children?"

"The Champ? He's not so bad."

"He's not so good, either."

Derek raised a hand to silence him. "Look, Mike—"

"I told you not to call me Mike!"

"All right,—Michael!" Derek corrected himself. "I appreciate your concern, but right now the kids aren't my problem. Evelyn is. How am I going to do what I have to do without hurting her?"

"I'm afraid I can't help you there," said Michael. "You were the one who asked for this."

"Like I need to be reminded. If only there were a way for me to stay with the kids and not hurt Evelyn."

"Actually," Michael began, "there *is* a way...."

Chapter Six

"And that is?"

"Love," Michael told him. "If you can find love, real love, while you're on Earth, if you can give it and receive it unconditionally, then you have a shot at another go-round down there."

"Love!" Derek snorted. "You couldn't get odds on it in Vegas."

"In your case, I wholeheartedly agree," said Michael, "which is why I hesitate to even discuss it with you."

"I swore off love, that kind of love, anyway, a long time ago," Derek said, still unable to shake the bitterness that had been Patricia's legacy to him.

Michael studied him for a long moment. "I know the Boss must have seen *some* redeeming qualities in you, or you wouldn't be here, even on a probationary basis, but for the life of me, I can't see any evidence of it except those kids."

"I like dogs," Derek said with a sarcastic edge in his voice.

"At least you like someone."

"I love my kids." Derek paused. "Look if you're finished with me, I really need to get back. It's almost dawn."

Michael nodded. "Sure."

Watching him go, Michael wondered if anyone—other than his kids—would ever penetrate that formidable barrier Derek Wolfe had erected around his heart. Though he'd never tell Derek, he suspected that beyond that barrier was a great deal of emotion. Powerful emotions. If anyone ever got through, it would make all the difference in the world.

If angels were allowed to bet, Michael's money would be on Evelyn Sloan.

"I'm sorry about last night," Evelyn told Derek over breakfast the next morning.

"You don't have anything to be sorry about," he responded, scooping up a bite of his western omelet and popping it into his mouth. "You said what you were feeling. Not all of us have that ability."

"That's not what I meant—"

"I understand," he assured her. "I haven't exactly been Mr. Wonderful. I know that. I had it coming."

"Yes, you did," she agreed with a nod. "But it was the wrong time."

He reached for his coffee. "How so?"

"You're at a disadvantage, Jeffrey," she pointed out. "You don't remember what it was like between us before. You only know about now. It's a brand-new relationship for you."

Literally, Derek was thinking.

"You're bound to have some reservations," she continued.

A textbook understatement if I ever heard one, he thought, but said nothing.

"I should have been a little more patient—no, I take that back. I should have been a lot more patient." She seemed embarrassed.

"Look, I'm sorry, Ev," he told her. "I know how hard this has been on you."

"On both of us," she corrected. "I love you, Jeff. I've always loved you. I want a future with you, and I'd like to believe that future is possible. But if you don't want it as much as I do, if you don't want it, period, I would rather you'd just tell me and get it over with than have you try to force it only to discover somewhere down the line that it's just not working—"

"Evelyn," he began, taking both of her hands in his, "don't go writing the eulogy while we're still breathing, okay?"

"Careful there, Derek."

"Michael. This is not a good time, in case you haven't noticed."

"There's no such thing as a good time where you're concerned."

"Let's get this over with, all right. What am I doing wrong this time?"

"You don't know?"

"I wasn't encouraging her."

"You would have."

"What are you, my conscience?"

"Someone has to be."

"What would you have me do? Tell her we don't have a snowball's chance in—a prayer of making it long-term?"

"You can't give her hope, then destroy her."

"I didn't make the rules, pal."

"Derek—"

"Jeffrey?"

Evelyn's voice brought him back to Earth abruptly. "I'm sorry," he apologized. "I guess my head was off in the clouds for a few minutes there."

"You scared me," Evelyn admitted. "I thought you were having some kind of epileptic seizure or something."

"It happens sometimes. I guess it's some sort of posttrauma thing. I don't know," he responded evasively.

"You were saying?"

"Huh?"

"Before you faded out, you were saying something about not writing us off." She picked absently at her food, most of which was still on her plate.

"Oh, yeah." He paused, waiting for Michael to object, but the senior angel was, for once, silent. "I was going to say, 'give it time.'"

Time, he was thinking. *Something I don't have.*

It's time for a change, Evelyn decided, studying her own reflection in the mirror.

She was even looking older these days. When she first met Jeffrey, she wore trendy clothes in bright colors and kept her hair long and loose, the way he'd always liked it. These days, her clothes were more functional than fashionable, and more often than not she tied her hair back in a ponytail to keep it out of her way. She couldn't remember how long it had been since she'd been to a party, since she'd danced all night.

How long had it been since she'd really enjoyed herself?

She got into her closet, trying on clothes she hadn't worn in ages, and it made her feel surprisingly good. It also made her wonder... wonder if she herself had been responsible for Jeffrey's waning interest in her. The woman he'd initially been attracted to didn't exist anymore. Jeffrey wasn't the kind of man who wanted stability. He'd never look for a woman who was a homebody. He didn't care if she could cook or not. No...Jeffrey wanted a woman who was sexy and fun, and he didn't believe stability and sexy could come in the same package. He wanted someone who liked to be on the go as much as he did, ready to fly off to San Francisco or Las Vegas or Barbados on a moment's notice, whether for a romantic weekend or just for dinner.

The way I used to be, Evelyn thought. But was that really me?

She wouldn't deny, especially to herself, that she enjoyed that life-style. For a time, anyway. When she met Jeffrey, he'd swept her off her feet with those spur-of-the-moment trips to glamorous and exotic places. Her head had definitely been turned by his surprises, especially those flights to other cities, just to have dinner or catch a show. But after a while, she'd found herself wanting something more.

Something Jeffrey obviously didn't want.

She thought about it. She wanted stability from him. She wanted commitment—emotionally *and* legally. He wanted her to be the adventurous, spirited woman he'd asked to marry him. Perhaps a compromise was in order, Evelyn concluded.

Perhaps if he were to fall in love with her all over again...

"I thought a picnic might be fun."

Derek couldn't hide his surprise. "A *picnic?*"

"You know, a blanket spread out on the grass, preferably under a large tree, a bottle of good wine, a big wicker hamper full of all kinds of good food—"

"And ants," he added.

"Ants—no. Ants would not dare ruin our picnic." She laughed.

"Do you know something the rest of us don't?" he asked, amused.

"Like what?"

"Like how to keep ants from gate-crashing a picnic."

"Intimidation," she told him. "That's the key."

He laughed. "You're in an awfully good mood today," he observed, charmed by her enthusiasm and high spirits.

"I'm turning over a new leaf."

"A new leaf?"

"Making a New Year's resolution," she offered in explanation.

"Wrong time of year," he pointed out.

"If you remember, we missed New Year's Eve," she said quietly, her mood suddenly serious.

He frowned. "One of the few things I *do* remember from before the accident," he admitted.

"We have a lot of catching up to do." She brightened again. "So, are you game?"

He grinned. "Sure. Why not?"

* * *

"The kids would have loved this place," Derek told Evelyn as they spread a blanket out on the grass under a huge oak tree. "We should have brought them along."

Evelyn tried to hide her puzzlement, and quickly denied the twinge of disappointment that made her feel so guilty. She loved the children. How could she feel jealousy toward them? "Next time," she promised.

On the lake at the bottom of the hill, not twenty yards away, mallard ducks and Canadian geese paddled lazily, waiting expectantly for any proffered crumbs from the yet-to-be-eaten picnic lunch. "A lot of people come here," Evelyn explained, "and everyone feeds them. It's like Pavlovian conditioning. They see a picnic hamper, they expect to be fed."

"Really?" He grinned. "Well, we can't disappoint them now, can we?"

Evelyn only smiled as she started to unpack the hamper. He worried about disappointing everyone, except her. Sometimes she wondered if he even realized he was disappointing her. But how could he *not* know?

"What've we got here?" he asked, peering into the hamper.

"All kinds of goodies," Evelyn said cheerfully. "Wine, three kinds of cheese, four kinds of crackers, bananas, kiwi fruit, grapes, peaches, seafood salad and bottled water."

"No steak and potatoes?" Derek asked.

She made a face. "Junk. Not at all healthy."

"I *like* steak and potatoes," he maintained.

"But they're not good for you. And you *are* still recovering."

"So you're giving me hospital food?"

"Jeffrey!"

"I *like* steak and potatoes," he repeated for emphasis.

"Give this stuff a chance, okay?" she urged. "Don't knock it till you've tried it."

"Did this stuff come from your restaurant?" he wanted to know.

"No, it came from my kitchen." She eyed him suspiciously. "Why do you ask?"

"You said I'd never liked the food from the restaurant," he recalled. "I figured maybe—"

"Oh, you louse!" She pushed him playfully. He fell back onto the blanket, pulling her with him. Lying on his back with her on top of him, eye to eye, they both started to laugh uncontrollably. Then, impulsively, Evelyn kissed him.

He returned the kiss freely, blown away by her spontaneity and the warmth of her, physically and emotionally. Then, abruptly, he withdrew.

"This isn't a good idea," he told her.

She sat up and stared at him, unable to hide her confusion. "What isn't a good idea?" she asked carefully.

"This. Us. Here." He waved his hand in frustration. "We *are* out in the open—"

"It never used to bother you before," she said irritably.

"It didn't? I mean—it didn't. I—I know it didn't," he stammered. "But things are different now."

"You can say that again."

"The doctor says it's too soon," he said, obviously embarrassed. "He says I'm not up to the physical stress yet."

"I didn't realize—" Evelyn began, equally embarrassed.

"I know," he said quickly. "I should have told you."

"Yes," she agreed, "you should have."

"I hated to admit it."

"Admit what? That you're temporarily incapacitated in certain ways?"

He didn't respond.

"It *is* temporary, isn't it?" she asked, concerned.

"As far as I know, yes."

"Well, then." She busied herself with the contents of the hamper. "Shall we eat? If you don't like it, I promise you steak and potatoes as soon as we get home...."

"You lied," Michael accused. "That's against the rules, and you know it!"

"Well, excuse me!" Derek responded crossly. "I'm really between a rock and a hard place here, you know. I'm supposed to be her fiancé, but I can't encourage her. I can't have a physical relationship with her, but I can't tell her why. I can't tell her the truth, but I can't lie. Tell me, Michael—what am I supposed to do?"

"Calm down, Derek—" Michael started.

"How am I supposed to handle this relationship?" he demanded. "How am I supposed to convince her I'm Jeffrey if I can't *act* like Jeffrey—"

His tirade was interrupted by a very loud clap of thunder. Michael frowned. "The Boss isn't very happy with you right now," he said in a worried tone.

"I'm not very happy with me, either," Derek said, suddenly subdued. "All I wanted to do was go back long enough to make sure Patrick and Alexandra were taken care of. I didn't want to get into this thing with Evelyn. I didn't want to get involved with her."

"But you are."

"I didn't say that."

"But you *are,*" Michael repeated.

"Stop putting words in my mouth!" Derek snapped.

"You wouldn't be so hypersensitive about this if you weren't feeling *something* for her," Michael pointed out. "Why won't you simply admit what you're feeling?"

"The last thing I need is to fall for a woman again," Derek grumbled. "Especially now."

"Correction. It may be the last thing you *want,*" said Michael, "but it's exactly what you need."

"Thank you, Dr. Freud," Derek responded sarcastically.

The truth hurt.

So much for sexy and fun.

Evelyn's frustration showed—in the expression on her face, in her uncharacteristic silence, in the way she handled the boxes in the restaurant storeroom. She knew she was too obvious, but she was unable to do anything about it.

"Want to talk about it?"

Evelyn turned. Sharon was standing in the doorway, watching her with concern. "Talk about what?" she asked, busying herself with the supplies that had just been delivered.

"Whatever it is that's making you abuse the tomatoes," Sharon said. "Or do I even have to ask what it's all about?"

"I don't know what you're talking about," Evelyn said irritably.

"What's Callander done now?" Sharon wanted to know.

Evelyn stopped what she was doing. "Why do you automatically assume Jeffrey is always the reason when I'm in a bad mood?" she asked, annoyed.

"I'm usually right, aren't I?" Sharon asked.

"I wish you'd give him a chance—"

"I think you've given him enough chances for both of us," Sharon argued. "And you still haven't answered my question. What's he done now?"

"He hasn't done anything. That's the problem." Evelyn shoved a large box onto the shelf above her with such force that the entire section of metal shelving shook violently.

"Meaning what exactly?" Sharon wasn't about to let it go.

Evelyn finally surrendered. "Okay. I've been thinking about what you said, about how much I've changed, about how I'm, as you put it, no fun anymore. I started thinking that if you had noticed it, Jeffrey must have, too."

"And?"

"I decided to do something about it."

"Like what?"

"I took a long, hard look at myself—my clothes, my hair, my life-style. I started thinking about the woman I was and the woman I've become." She paused. "I could see how he could have lost interest in me."

Sharon selected a ripe banana from a nearby open crate and peeled it slowly. "Too bad you didn't lose interest in him," she commented.

Evelyn ignored the remark. "I decided to dress and act like the old Evelyn again," she went on.

"Trying to turn him on," Sharon concluded.

"Something like that, yes."

"And?"

"We went on a picnic. I'd planned it all so carefully. I wanted it to be perfect," she said. "It *was* perfect. He was laughing and playful, and we started kissing."

"So far, so good," Sharon acknowledged. "So what went wrong?"

"He couldn't..."

"What?"

"He couldn't make love to me," Evelyn admitted, embarrassed.

"Couldn't—or wouldn't?" Sharon asked.

"Couldn't."

"Well, I'll be—" Sharon howled with laughter.

"It's not funny!"

"Maybe not to you, but—" Sharon couldn't stop laughing. "—how about that? There *is* justice in this world, after all."

"I shouldn't have told you," Evelyn said regretfully.

"I'm sorry," Sharon apologized, realizing how painful this was for her sister. "But the idea of good old Jeffrey being incapacitated is...well...delicious."

"I can't talk to you about this!" Frustrated, Evelyn pushed past her sister and left the restaurant.

"The circus is in town, you know."

The children were enthusiastic, wildly enthusiastic,

in their response. "You'd take us to the circus?" Patrick asked.

"Sure I would," Derek said, grinning. "I love the circus."

"And I love you, Jeff!" Alexandra crawled onto his lap and gave him a hug.

Derek couldn't hold back the tears of joy that sprang to his eyes. How he'd missed holding his children like this. He found himself recalling the last time Alexandra had crawled up on his lap for a hug....

"Get a move on, guys!" he called out to them as he put breakfast on the table. "I've got to run."

He'd meant that literally. He ran, at least three miles, every morning before leaving for his job as a marketing executive. That was as close to engaging in a sport as he'd ever been. He wasn't putting his physical safety on the line for the sake of winning. After all, he had two kids to think about.

Two kids without a mother.

Being a single parent was an enormous responsibility, even more so than being one of two parents. But Derek also found it rewarding. And he had to admit, if only to himself, that he was better satisfied without Patricia there to cast a dark cloud over their existence.

It had been rough on the kids for a while. He'd put them both in therapy right after she left. He smiled to himself. Their therapist had been a young woman named Prudence whose name seemed to suit her perfectly. But she'd done his kids a world of good, so he'd refrained from making fun of her overly straitlaced appearance and manner. And their housekeeper, Mrs. Anderson, had supplied lots of warmth and hugs.

"What's for breakfast?" Patrick wanted to know as he raced into the kitchen and climbed onto his chair.

"Waffles, with peaches," Derek told him.

"Yum!" Patrick attacked his plate with the gusto of someone who hadn't eaten in a month, but then, that was the usual approach his son took to food. Derek was surprised that the boy never seemed to gain any weight.

"What's for lunch?" Patrick asked then, eyeing the lunch boxes on the counter.

Derek laughed. "Pat, only you would ask what's for lunch while you're still eating breakfast," he told his son.

"You usually give us better stuff than they got at the preschool," Patrick told him, taking a big bite.

"Well, today you have ham-and-cheese sandwiches, oranges and Twinkies," Derek said.

"Twinkies!" Alexandra cheered happily as she came into the kitchen. "I love Twinkies."

"I know you do, sweetheart," Derek said with a wink as he pulled up a chair and put on his running shoes. "Listen, guys, I'm going out for my morning run," he told them. "I'll be back in a little while, okay? In the meantime, be good for Mrs. Anderson."

"Don't go, Daddy!" Alexandra flew into his arms, looking up at him like a small, frightened animal as she hugged him tightly.

"Hey, what's this?" Derek wanted to know. "I run every day. Why is today different?"

"If you go, you won't come back!" she sobbed.

"Sure, I will," he answered her. "I always do, don't I?"

After she finally calmed down, Derek thought it over. He considered skipping his run for a day, but decided that wasn't a good idea. He had to prove to her that there was nothing to be afraid of.

He had to go.

It started out just like every other morning run. Uneventful. It was sunny and warm, warmer than it had been the past few days. Not a cloud in the sky, and not much in the way of traffic, at least not at this time of the morning. He kept a steady pace, even as he waved at the people he saw along the way, the same people he saw every morning.

He never saw the diaper-service truck.

The driver of the truck hadn't seen him, either, until it was too late. Derek had cut between two parked cars, crossing the street in the middle rather than at the end of the block as he should have, anxious to get home, to prove to his daughter that there was nothing to worry about.

Alexandra, he thought as his spirit left his broken body. Oh, dear God—Alexandra!

Chapter Seven

Evelyn was still shaking when she parked her car and sat there for a long time, not getting out even though she was in her own driveway.

She couldn't take any more of this.

She should have known better than to try to talk to Sharon about the situation. Sharon wouldn't be sympathetic. Sharon didn't like Jeffrey and never had. Nothing would make her happier than to see Evelyn end her relationship with him.

Evelyn wished she knew what was going on with him. She wished she understood why he was acting so strangely. She wished she knew what, if anything, he wanted from her. But then, thinking back, he'd always been unpredictable, even when things were good between them. . . .

"Where are we going?" she had asked.

"It's a surprise," Jeffrey had responded evasively.

PLAY
ONE MILLION
BIG BUCKS
ONE MILLION
AND YOU COULD WIN THE
$1,000,000.00
PLUS JACKPOT!
SILHOUETTE
YOUR PERSONAL GAME CARD INSIDE . . .

IT'S FUN!

IT'S FREE!

HOW TO PLAY

BIG BUCKS

It's so easy...grab a lucky coin, and go right to your BIG BUCKS game card. Scratch off silver squares in a STRAIGHT LINE (across, down, or diagonal) until 5 dollar signs are revealed. BINGO....Doing this makes you eligible for a chance to win $1,000,000.00 in lifetime income ($33,333.33 each year for 30 years)! Also scratch all 4 corners to reveal the dollar signs. This entitles you to a chance to win the $50,000.00 Extra Bonus Prize! Void if more than 9 squares scratched off.

Your EXCLUSIVE PRIZE NUMBER is in the upper right corner of your game card. Return your game card and we'll activate your unique Sweepstakes Number, so it's important that your name and address section is completed correctly. This will permit us to identify you and match you with any cash prize rightfully yours! (SEE BACK OF BOOK FOR DETAILS.)

FREE BOOKS PLUS FREE GIFTS!

At the same time you play your BIG BUCKS game card for BIG CASH PRIZES...scratch the Lucky Charm to receive FOUR FREE

Silhouette Romance™ novels, and a FREE GIFT, TOO! They're totally free, absolutely free with no obligation to buy anything!

These books have a cover price of $2.75 each. But THEY ARE TOTALLY FREE; even the shipping will be at our expense! The Silhouette Reader Service™ is not like some book clubs. You don't have to buy any minimum number of purchases–not even one!

The fact is, thousands of readers look forward to receiving six of the best new romance novels each month and they love our discount prices!

Of course you may play BIG BUCKS for cash prizes alone by not scratching off your Lucky Charm, but why not get everything that we are offering and that you are entitled to! You'll be glad you did.

Offer limited to one per household and not valid to current Silhouette Romance® subscribers. All orders subject to approval.

TWO WAYS TO WIN BIG BUCKS!

1. Uncover 5 $ signs in a row . . . BINGO! You're eligible to win the $1,000,000.00 SWEEPSTAKES!

2. Uncover 5 $ signs in a row AND uncover $ signs in all 4 corners . . . BINGO! You're also eligible for the $50,000.00 EXTRA BONUS PRIZE!

LUCKY CHARM GAME!

Claim 3 FREE Books AND a FREE Mystery Gift!

Scratch here ☞

HURRY! *This jackpot must be claimed!*

YES! I have played my BIG BUCKS game card as instructed. Enter my Big Bucks Prize number in the MILLION DOLLAR Sweepstakes III and also enter me for the Extra Bonus Prize. When winners are selected, tell me if I've won. If the Lucky Charm is scratched off, I will also receive everything revealed, as explained on the back of this page.

215 CIS ANTK
(U-SIL-R-05/94)

NAME _____

ADDRESS _____ APT. _____

CITY _____ STATE _____ ZIP _____

NO PURCHASE OR OBLIGATION NECESSARY TO ENTER SWEEPSTAKES.

© 1993 HARLEQUIN ENTERPRISES LTD.   PRINTED IN U.S.A.

EXCLUSIVE PRIZE # 4M 7737٤٤

BIG BUCKS

$

That much had been obvious. When he'd called her that day, just over a year ago, he refused to tell her where they were going. All he would say was that she should dress formally. He'd picked her up in a limousine, and promptly blindfolded her.

"What's this all about?" she had demanded to know.

He'd only laughed. "You'll find out," he promised.

"When?"

"Soon enough, my dear," he assured her. "Soon enough."

When they finally stopped and he helped her out of the car, she could have sworn they were at the airport. She started to remove the blindfold, but he stopped her.

"Not yet," he said.

"When?" This was driving her crazy.

"In time."

"How much time?"

He'd laughed. "Don't be so impatient," he growled. "You'll ruin everything."

He led her up what seemed to be a very long flight of stairs, but even with his assistance, she'd tripped twice. "This isn't funny, Callander," she complained.

"That, my sweet, depends upon your viewpoint." He chuckled.

Only when she felt the strong vibration of the craft taking off and heard the pilot speak to Jeffrey over the speakers did she confirm to herself that they had indeed been at the airport, and that they were now on his private plane, taking off for God only knew where.

"I want to take the blindfold off, Jeffrey," she told him again.

"Not yet."

"Jeffrey—"

"Humor me," he told her. "I promise you, the surprise I have for you will be worth it."

"It had better be."

"Is that a threat?" he asked, feigning shock.

"Call it a promise."

"I'm wounded," he told her with mock hurt in his voice. "You don't trust me."

"I never know what to expect from you."

It was true, then and now.

Evelyn's thoughts returned to the present. That night, their destination had been Los Angeles and a late supper at Spago. There had been other impromptu getaways, as well: lunch in San Francisco, at a wonderful restaurant overlooking the Bay; that weekend in Las Vegas at the Excalibur. He'd been so impulsive, so unpredictable.

He was still unpredictable, but in a much more disconcerting way.

"Jeff's taking us to the circus," Patrick announced over dinner.

Evelyn was surprised. "The circus?" she asked. "Are you sure?"

"That's what he said."

"He's getting tickets," Alexandra told her.

"When?"

"Right away."

"No. I mean, when is he taking you?" Evelyn wanted to know.

"Oh, this weekend," Patrick answered.

Jeffrey hadn't said a word to her about it, and it made her angry. He could have asked her before making any promises. He could have checked to see if she already had plans.

But then, he obviously hadn't planned to ask her to join them.

He'd done a complete turnaround. He adored the children, went out of his way to spend time with them. She would have been thrilled about that—if he weren't now avoiding her.

"We can go, can't we?"

Patrick's words cut through her thoughts. "What?"

"It's okay for us to go to the circus with Jeff, isn't it?" Patrick asked, suddenly concerned.

"Sure," Evelyn said with a sigh. What could she say, after all? If she said no, the kids would be deeply disappointed. They'd probably think her an ogre, especially since she'd been trying for months to get them to connect with him. He would no doubt find it odd, as well. Would he think she was jealous?

She thought she was.

"Why don't you just admit it?" Michael asked.

"Admit what?" Derek asked.

"That you do have feelings for Evelyn Sloan."

"Of course I have feelings for her," Derek snapped crossly. "She's a wonderful woman and a terrific foster mother for my kids."

"I'm talking about other feelings," Michael clarified. "The kind of feelings a man has for a woman— love, physical desire—"

"Physical desire?" Derek scowled at him. "I'm not dead—"

"Yes, you are," Michael reminded him.

"She's an attractive woman," Derek said.

Michael nodded. "Yes, she is."

"She's also very warm and caring."

"Definitely."

"She's intelligent."

"Very."

"She's independent."

"Yes."

"And successful."

"A self-made woman."

"There's a lot about her to admire."

"I agree," Michael said without hesitation. "There's also a lot to love."

"I'm not in love with her!" Derek snapped.

But as Michael watched Derek descend through the clouds, he knew. Derek was falling in love with Evelyn Sloan, even though he still refused to admit it, even to himself. It was unfortunate his ex-wife still caused him to hold back.

Opening his heart could mean a whole new life for him, literally.

"Patrick and Alexandra tell me you're taking them to the circus," Evelyn mentioned to Derek later that evening.

He looked embarrassed. "I know I should have talked to you about it first, but it wasn't something I'd planned," he told her. "It came up unexpectedly."

"So I hear."

"You're welcome to come, too," he said quickly.

Though it may not have been intentional on his part, to Evelyn, his suggestion felt like an afterthought, and it hurt. "I don't know," she said carefully. "I'll let you know."

"Sure."

He was pulling away from her, even more so than he had before his accident. They were like strangers now. He was a warmer, more caring man than he'd been before, but the more time he spent with her, the more distant he was. It was as if he was afraid to be close to her.

"Everyone's been asking when we're going to set a date," she said aloud.

"A date?"

"A wedding date."

"Oh. What have you told them?" he asked.

"That it's too soon, that we haven't really had much of a chance to talk about it."

"Good answer."

"Is it?"

He gave her a puzzled look.

"I've been giving this a lot of thought," she began carefully. "So much has happened. There's so much you don't remember."

He looked concerned. "I know you haven't been happy with me since I came home, Evelyn—"

"I think the problem is that you haven't been happy with me," Evelyn responded honestly.

"That's not true."

"Please don't lie to me, Jeff," she said sadly. "I'm not blind, and the way you've changed is glaringly obvious."

"The accident—" he began, openly upset.

She nodded. "I know that the accident is part of it, yes, but I think there's more."

"Evelyn—"

"Please, Jeffrey, let me finish," she said firmly. "I think having been so close to death made you realize how fragile, how short life really is. I think you woke up to realize there was a lot you still wanted to do with your life, and I didn't fit into your plans.''

''That's not exactly true—'' Derek began.

''Or maybe you just can't commit to our relationship now because you don't really remember me or what we had together,'' she continued. ''But what if that memory never returns?''

''We could start all over again,'' he suggested.

''We could, yes,'' she said. ''But do you really want to?''

''I—''

''Don't answer right now, Jeffrey.'' She cut him off. ''Think about it. Make sure it's what you really want before we go any further.''

He nodded, avoiding her eyes.

''I'll accept whatever you decide,'' she promised.

''Can I still see the kids?'' he asked.

This is weird, Evelyn thought.

Before the accident, he'd been ready to call off the wedding because she wanted to be a mother. When Patrick and Alexandra came to live with her, he'd gone to incredible lengths to avoid spending any time with them. Now, he was worried about being able to see them.

It was like a soap opera.

If Evelyn didn't know better, she'd think he'd awakened from the coma to the discovery that he was Patrick and Alexandra's real, biological father. But knowing that wasn't possible, Evelyn also knew there had to be something going on with him that he wasn't willing to share with her, something she hadn't been able to figure out on her own.

Nothing about Jeffrey made any sense anymore.

She didn't want to end their relationship. But as much as she had once loved Jeffrey, as much as she had wanted a future with him, she was more certain than ever that they didn't stand a chance.

They didn't have a prayer.

"She wants to end it," Derek told Michael.

"So, why are you complaining?" Michael asked. "This should certainly make things easier for you."

"How do you figure?"

"You're satisfied that your children are in good hands, aren't you?"

"Yes."

"And you don't want what anyone would call a 'serious relationship' with the lady, do you?"

"Well, no."

"So what's the problem?"

"I still have time left. I'd like to spend as much of it as possible with my kids."

"She won't let you see them?" Michael asked.

"I didn't say that."

"Did she?"

"Not yet."

"But you think she will."

"I think she might."

"Why?"

"Why would she allow me to see Patrick and Alexandra if we call it quits?" Derek asked. "If there's no marriage, Jeffrey Callander won't be a part of their lives."

"I see."

"I blew it, didn't I?"

"Like a hurricane."

* * *

"What part of the circus do you like best, Jeff?" Patrick wanted to know.

Derek pretended to give it a great deal of thought. "I guess I like the clowns best," he said finally.

"I like the trapeze guys," Patrick said promptly.

"I like the clowns," Alexandra said.

Derek had gotten the best seats in the house, front row, center ring. He bought the kids everything they asked for, and as a result was loaded down with balloons, sodas, popcorn, hot dogs and cotton candy. It reminded him of their past outings—when he was "Daddy" instead of "Jeff."

He missed those days so much, but they were lost to him forever.

"Here come the elephants!" Patrick yelled.

"All right!" Alexandra, excited by the sight of them, promptly dumped her soda down the front of Derek's shirt.

He only laughed. It wasn't the first time, and he suspected it wouldn't be the last. He hoped it wouldn't be the last. He'd missed doing things with his kids, even when it meant a huge cleaning bill. He appreciated those times even more now than he had before.

"Look at the horses!" Alexandra squealed with delight.

"There're the clowns, Alex!" Patrick told her.

"Wheee!" The popcorn went the way of the soda. Fortunately for Derek, it wasn't as sticky. Not that it would have mattered to Derek.

He was in Heaven—emotionally if not literally.

Thinking about it now for the first time in a very long time, he couldn't remember Patricia doing things like this with them. She hadn't done much of anything with them since they were babies and she began to lose interest in motherhood. He remembered one of the many arguments they'd had about it.

"Have you forgotten that you have two children, Patricia?" he'd demanded to know.

"How could I forget?" Her tone was sarcastic. "You keep reminding me."

"They're yours—your own flesh and blood," he argued. "Don't you care at all about them?"

"I'm not cut out to be a mother, Derek," she told him honestly. "Unfortunately, I came to that conclusion a bit too late."

"So, you're just going to turn your back on them as if they're unwanted pets or something?" he asked angrily.

"It's not as if they're being abandoned, Derek," she pointed out. "They have you."

"They need a mother."

"Well, *I* can't be the kind of mother they need!" she'd retorted.

Derek's thoughts returned to the present. He still found it hard to believe she had been able to turn her back on them so easily, to just walk out on them as if they meant nothing to her.

But she had.

Evelyn cried herself to sleep.

Jeffrey brought the kids home later than expected, later than she had told him to have them home. She hadn't had the opportunity to discuss it, or anything else, with him, though. He hadn't come in when he brought them home. He sat in his car in the driveway and watched until they were safely inside.

He hadn't come to the door because he hadn't wanted to see her.

It's over, she thought. It's really over.

She thought about how things had been between them before the accident—the good times and the bad, how she had stayed by his side after the accident, until he came out of the coma, so certain he was going to be all right, refusing to give up on him.

For what, she asked herself. For this?

She hated having such mean-spirited thoughts. She certainly didn't want anything bad to happen to Jeffrey, regardless of how their relationship turned out.

Life could be so unfair....

Derek wasn't sleeping very well, either.

But unlike Evelyn, he wasn't quite sure *why* he was unable to sleep. He told himself he should be happy. He should be satisfied. His kids were in good hands. They had a foster mother who adored them and would give them a good life. They would never forget him, but in time they would be happy, truly happy. He could return to Heaven with that knowledge.

So what was bothering him now?

Evelyn. He was thinking about Evelyn, about how badly he'd hurt her. It bothered him more than he had expected it to. After Patricia, he thought his heart had been hardened enough to women—all women—to prevent him from feeling any regret, no matter how much he might have caused her. But it mattered to him that he had hurt Evelyn. It mattered that he was the cause of her unhappiness.

Could Michael be right?

He dismissed the thought as quickly as it had come to him. He cared about Evelyn, yes, but he was not in love with her. He wasn't in love with any woman and never would be again.

I'll never be that stupid again, he promised himself.

Evelyn was a wonderful woman—warm and caring and giving—but so was Patricia before their marriage. Evelyn was a career woman, like Patricia—how important was that restaurant to her? The kids came first with her, but where would a husband figure into her priorities?

And why did it matter to him, one way or the other?

"I don't get it, no. Suppose you explain it to me."

Derek frowned. "I don't know why it's so hard to understand," he began. "I'd like to take the kids for the weekend. I'd like to take them camping. I'd like your permission to take them."

"Why camping?"

"Why not?"

"No, I mean, why would you think of taking them camping?" she asked.

He shrugged. "Most kids enjoy that sort of thing."

She gave him an accusing look. "But *you* don't," she told him.

"I don't?"

"This makes no sense at all to me, Jeffrey," she told him. "Before the accident, you wanted no part of fatherhood. You were furious with me for deciding to become a foster mother. You avoided spending time with the children whenever possible."

"Evelyn—"

"Now you can't spend enough time with them," she continued. "You're not only doing things with them, you're doing things you've always hated. You took them to a wrestling match—you always said wrestling was nothing more than a cheap, badly acted stage show."

"So I was wrong."

"You took them to the circus. You've never liked circuses or amusement parks *or* carnivals," she told him.

"I never wanted to relive my childhood."

She gave him a puzzled look. "Why?"

"I just didn't," he answered evasively.

"Now you want to take them camping."

"I didn't realize camping was illegal."

"It was as far as you were concerned," she shot back at him. "You hated camping. You hated bugs and cooking over an open fire and sleeping on the ground and not having telephones and electricity and central air-conditioning."

"I'll try anything once," he maintained.

"Do you want to be their father?" she asked then, impulsively.

He looked at her as though he'd been physically struck. "What?"

She repeated the question. "Do you want to be their father?"

His mind was racing. He didn't know where her question was coming from, but he was caught between a rock and a hard place. He obviously couldn't tell her the truth, but Michael had made it clear that he couldn't lie to her, either. "Where is this coming from?" he wanted to know.

"I don't know," she admitted. "All I know is that nothing else makes any sense. First, you wanted no part of fatherhood or children, then you do this complete turnaround and become a model daddy and the kids adore you and—"

"Anyone can change, Evelyn," he pointed out.

"That dramatically? Please!" She wasn't buying it for a minute.

"Miracles do still happen."

"Well, that one would rank right up there with the parting of the Red Sea!" she snapped.

"Where did you get the idea that I want to be their father?" he asked carefully.

"It's the only explanation that makes any sense."

"How so?"

"It would explain the change in you."

"Evelyn, this doesn't make any sense—"

"You can say that again." Frustrated and angry, she turned and walked out, leaving him staring after her.

"What do you think I should have done?" Derek asked irritably.

Michael's face remained impassive. "She didn't have a clue, you know," he said quietly.

"Yeah?"

Michael nodded. "She didn't suspect you *were* the children's father."

Derek frowned. "What made her even bring it up?" he wanted to know.

"She's desperate. Surely that comes as no great surprise to you," Michael stated.

Derek shook his head. It didn't.

"She's confused and frightened. The man she was planning to marry has changed dramatically and she can't find a logical explanation for it," Michael pointed out. "She sees only that she's losing him, and she feels powerless to do anything about it."

"I've got a major problem here, Michael," Derek told him. "I'm not allowed to lie to her—"

"Not an outright lie, no," Michael agreed.

"But I'm living a lie! I'm not really Jeffrey Callander!"

Michael shrugged. "I told you it wouldn't be easy."

After a long silence, Derek spoke again. "I'm curious about something," he began.

"And that is?"

"You."

"What about me?"

"You haven't been, uh, here very long. How'd you get to be a senior angel so quickly?" Derek asked.

Michael smiled for the first time. "My heart was in the right place," he said simply.

"Stupid, stupid, stupid!"

Evelyn wasn't quite sure who or what she envisioned on the chopping block in front of her as she continued to whack at the meat with unnecessary force. Maybe no one in particular. Maybe she was just venting frustration in general.

Why had she ever asked Jeffrey such a stupid question? She could imagine how she must have sounded to him, like a silly, insecure female. The last thing she wanted to sound like.

"Anybody I know?"

Evelyn looked up to see Sharon coming into the kitchen. "I don't want to talk about it," she said sharply.

"Ah," Sharon responded with a nod and a knowing smile. "Must have something to do with Jeffrey, right?"

Evelyn gave the meat another whack. "I said I don't want to talk about it."

Sharon was silent for a moment. "Look…I'm sorry if I've hurt you or upset you with some of the things I've said," she began, leaning on one corner of the table on which Evelyn was working. "I've only butted in because I care. I don't want to see you hurt any more than you already have been."

"I know that, but—"

They were interrupted by the ringing telephone. "I'll get it," Sharon volunteered. She picked it up, speaking only for a moment before passing the receiver to her sister.

"Who is it?" Evelyn asked.

"Your knight in tarnished armor."

Chapter Eight

"Jeffrey?"

Sharon frowned, almost scowled. "Unfortunately."

Evelyn took the phone. "Jeffrey? What—"

"We need to talk, Evelyn."

She hesitated. "Do we have anything left to talk about?" she asked dubiously.

"I think we do. Don't you?"

"I don't know."

"Will you at least hear what I have to say?"

She thought about it, deciding it couldn't hurt. "I'm listening," she said aloud.

"Not over the phone."

"Where, then?"

"Dinner, tonight," he told her. "I'll pick you up at eight."

"I'm not sure—" she began.

He didn't give her a chance to refuse. "I'll pick you up at eight," he repeated.

Then he hung up.

Evelyn turned to Sharon, who looked at her questioningly. "Well?"

"He wants to talk, that's all."

"I'll bet."

Evelyn drew in a deep breath. "I'm not going to get into this with you, Sharon," she said wearily. "You're my sister and I love you dearly, but you can't stand Jeffrey and you don't understand what I'm feeling."

She wasn't sure she understood it herself.

"Are you going to see Jeff tonight?"

Alexandra had wandered into Evelyn's bedroom while Evelyn was dressing for dinner, and was sitting cross-legged in the middle of the bed, playing with a long strand of faux pearls Evelyn had left on the dressing table.

"Yes, I am." Evelyn checked her reflection in the full-length mirror on the closet door, then turned to look at the child. "You really like Jeff, don't you?" she asked.

Alexandra nodded, grinning broadly. "A lot."

"He's good to you, isn't he?" Evelyn asked.

Alexandra nodded again.

"You have a good time with him?"

"You bet. He does things with us. Things like we used to do with Daddy." Alexandra fingered the pearls as she talked, examining them with fascination.

"You'd miss him if he went away, wouldn't you?" Evelyn asked, trying to keep her tone casual.

Alexandra looked alarmed. "He's *not* going away, is he?" she asked with a sudden urgency in her voice.

Evelyn sat on the bed beside her. "Honey, I don't think Jeffrey would ever intentionally go away," she began, trying to offer the little girl comfort, but not at all sure what Jeffrey might or might not do.

"Daddy went away!" Alexandra wailed.

"Oh, sweetheart." Evelyn held her close. "Jeffrey's not going away the same way your father did."

But, she thought sadly, it could be just as final.

And just as painful.

"The kids really love you," Evelyn revealed over dinner.

"I love them, too," he responded without hesitation. "They're great kids."

She shook her head, smiling. "You know, it still amazes me," she admitted.

"What?"

"The way you've changed toward the kids," she said. "I think it qualifies as a minor miracle at the very least."

He shrugged. "I just woke up to what I was missing out on," he said simply.

"Alexandra was upset this evening," she told him then.

"Oh?" He reached for his drink. "About what?"

"About you," she said. "She's afraid you'll 'go away' one day the same way her father did."

He frowned. "That never occurred to me," he said, obviously concerned.

"I beg your pardon?"

"I never thought about how it would affect them."

"What?"

"Getting close to them, leaving them vulnerable to the risk of losing someone again," he told her.

"I beg your pardon?"

He seemed hesitant at first. "You've already made it clear you've decided to end this relationship," he reminded her. "I assume if you're serious, that would mean my relationship with the children would end."

"Well, yes."

"This also isn't going to help your chances of getting permanent custody," he pointed out.

"You don't have to remind me of that," she said sullenly.

"What are you going to do?" he asked.

"I wish I knew."

"Mind if I make a suggestion?" he asked.

She frowned. "At this point I'm willing to consider just about anything," she admitted.

"You and I loved each other, right? We were going to be married before my accident?"

"Jeffrey—"

"Hear me out," he urged. "I know things haven't been right between us since I came home, that I'm not the same man you fell in love with, that I may never be. But we could try, couldn't we?"

"I don't know, Jeffrey. I just don't know."

"Consider it, Evelyn. If not for us, then for the children," he told her.

She didn't bother to mask her surprise. "The children?"

"You could get permanent custody if we were married."

Evelyn was stunned. "Are you suggesting we get married just so I can get permanent custody of the children?" she asked carefully.

"Not just for that reason, no."

"Are you saying you love me?" she asked.

"I'm saying love is a big part of this. I'm saying it's worth a try," he said.

There was a time Evelyn would have agreed, but now she wasn't so sure.

"What were you thinking of?" Michael demanded angrily. "You asked her to marry you. You can't marry her."

"Why not?"

"Because you're only there on a temporary basis," Michael reminded him. "Because you're not Jeffrey Callander."

"Look, Michael, I went back to make sure my kids were in good hands, that they'd be growing up secure, with someone who could love them as much as I do. As unfair as it is, without a husband Evelyn may lose custody of them."

"I see," Michael said with a nod. "You're doing this for your children, then?"

"Well, yes."

"And what does Evelyn Sloan get out of it?"

"A husband."

"A husband who doesn't love her," Michael said. "A husband who's going to die in less than a month."

"A husband who's going to leave her with a nice fat inheritance," Derek reminded him.

Michael shot him a disapproving look.

"I believe that's the way Jeffrey would want it," Derek said in his own defense.

"I'm sure you're right, but I don't believe it will compensate for the pain you're causing her," Michael told him.

"So what am I supposed to do?" Derek asked, frustrated.

"I don't think you're going to have much choice."

"Meaning exactly what?"

"Meaning the Boss may call you back."

"Call me back?" Derek couldn't believe it.

"You went too far," Michael told him. "You've done everything, virtually everything, you were told *not* to do."

"I've done whatever was necessary for the sake of my kids!" Derek insisted.

"You are not allowed to hurt other people to accomplish your goals, no matter how noble those goals might be," Michael reminded him.

"If I marry her, I'll be securing her future, too," Derek maintained.

It was clear that Michael was losing patience with him. "Has it occurred to you that all the money in the world won't repair the damage you're doing to her emotionally?" he demanded.

"She'll get over it."

"Really. You didn't," Michael reminded him.

"Now wait a minute—"

"It's the truth, whether you're willing to admit it to yourself or not," Michael said. "You won't let yourself care for any woman because of what Patricia did to you, but what you're doing to Evelyn now is just as despicable."

"I have to do what's best for my kids!"

"You have to respect the rules!" Michael snapped back at him. "If you don't, you'll be recalled."

"I can't—"

"This is the last warning you're going to get, Derek."

There was a finality in Michael's voice that left no doubt in Derek's mind that it was not an empty threat.

* * *

Evelyn didn't know what to do.

She'd loved Jeffrey once. She'd wanted to marry him. Seven months ago, she wouldn't have had to think about it. She would have married him in a New York minute. But so much had happened . . . so much had gone wrong between them. So much about him, about the current state of their relationship confused her. And now . . .

Now, he again wanted to marry her.

No "I love you," no "I can't live without you," no "I need you." No passion, no fireworks. Just a simple proposition, for the sake of the children.

For the sake of the children, she thought. Children he was never with for more than ten minutes at a time before his accident. Children he's suddenly playing doting daddy to.

It doesn't make sense.

I'm entering into a marriage of convenience, she thought. But I loved him once. And I wanted it to work so badly then.

She'd tried. Heaven knew she'd tried.

"You're going to do what?"

"I'm going to marry Jeffrey," Evelyn told her sister again, though she knew Sharon had heard her the first time.

"Are you nuts?"

Evelyn gave her a tired smile. "The jury's still out on that one," she told Sharon, checking the contents of the large refrigerators to make sure the restaurant wasn't running low of anything important.

"He's made you miserable ever since he came home from the hospital—no, before that, even. How can

you even think about marrying him?'' Sharon asked
with alarm.

"I love him," Evelyn insisted.

"Love him? Jeez!" Sharon threw up her hands in
exasperation. "How can you love that louse?"

"We can't help who we fall in love with," Evelyn
said.

"I know they say love is blind," Sharon began,
"but in your case, sis, I think it must be brain-dead."

"Thank you for your vote of confidence," Evelyn
said darkly.

"You know what I mean," Sharon responded.

"Sometimes I wonder."

Sharon was silent for a long time. "You're doing
this for the kids, aren't you?" she finally asked.

Evelyn stiffened. "What makes you say that?"

"Come on, sis," Sharon responded. "When he first
came home from the hospital, you were gushing about
how wonderful he was, how much he'd changed, how
terrific he was with the kids."

"He was."

"Then it all started to sour," Sharon remembered.
"He was great with the kids but cool with you."

"He's been through a lot, Sharon."

"So have you."

"It's not the same."

"You never answered my question."

"What question?"

"You are doing this for the kids, aren't you?"

"Sharon—"

"I know how much those kids mean to you, Ev,"
Sharon said then. "I know how worried you've been
since social services they told you there might be a

problem in getting permanent custody of Patrick and Alexandra.''

Evelyn didn't respond. The truth hurt.

"Funny," Evelyn began, "but I always thought when I decided to get married, it would be very different from this.''

"Different, how?" Derek asked, not sure he really wanted to hear her answer.

"For one thing, more romantic,'' she said with an unmistakable twinge of sadness in her voice.

He attempted to reassure her. "I'm trying Ev."

She forced a smile. "Not exactly Romeo and Juliet, are we?'' she observed.

"We were once."

She shook her head. "We were more like Tracy and Hepburn than Romeo and Juliet.''

He grinned. "Well, I promise to try to be more Romeo-like in the future,'' he vowed.

She laughed at that. "I don't think you could be Romeo-like to save your life," she told him.

He didn't respond. She didn't know it, couldn't know it, but that was exactly what he was doing.

"What kind of wedding do you want?" she asked then.

"I'll leave that up to you."

Tucking a pencil behind her ear, she looked up at him questioningly. "You don't have a preference?"

He shrugged. "Don't most men prefer the small, Las Vegas-type quickie weddings?''

She grimaced. "Is that what you want?"

"I want you to be happy," he told her. "The wedding day should be the bride's day, after all. It's your choice.''

"How many people do you want to invite? Your friends, I mean?" she asked.

"Nobody."

"Nobody?"

He nodded. "Nobody."

"No family, no friends?"

He shook his head. "I don't have any family. You know that," he said. "And I don't have any friends to speak of. At least not the kind I'd want at my wedding."

She gave him a little smile. "I think we'd better make it a small wedding," she decided. "There aren't that many people I want to invite, either."

"Well, you can still have a formal wedding if you want," he said, "even if it is small."

Evelyn nodded. "That would be nice."

"I think it would be nicer than a big formal wedding."

"So do I."

"You could still have your long white dress."

"Maybe a candlelight ceremony. I could arrange it for next week," she considered.

"That would be nice."

"I'd like to have Sharon as my maid of honor, but she'd probably show up dressed in black," Evelyn speculated.

"I'd like the kids to be a part of our wedding," Derek told her.

She nodded. "Patrick can be the ring bearer and Alexandra the flower girl," she agreed.

"I think they'd like that," he said.

"I know they would," she said. Then, after a long pause she said, "You know, there was a time I thought the children would consider our marriage a catastrophe ranking right up there with the end of the world."

"And now?"

"Now I think they're going to be thrilled."

"Let's tell them tonight," he urged.

"Must be serious," Patrick said, looking up at them, "if you have to tell us together."

Evelyn knelt so that she was as close as possible to the child's eye level. "It is serious," she acknowledged, "but I hope it's news that will make both of you very happy."

"What is it?" Patrick asked.

"Evelyn and I are getting married," Derek told them.

"We're going to be a real family. We've also made plans to start the adoption process," Evelyn added.

"All right!" Patrick cheered.

"Hooray!" Alexandra cried out happily.

"I take it they're happy about it," Derek said to Evelyn.

She smiled. "I think you may be right."

"When are you going to get married?" Patrick asked them.

Evelyn and Derek settled onto the couch, side by side. "We want to do it as soon as possible," Evelyn said.

"And we'd like both of you to be a part of the wedding," Derek told them.

Both children gave him a quizzical look.

"We thought you could serve as our ring bearer and flower girl," Evelyn explained.

"Would I have to wear a suit?" Patrick asked.

"A tuxedo," Derek told him.

The boy made a face. "Yuck!"

"Will I get to wear a long dress?" Alexandra wanted to know.

"Very long," Evelyn promised. "Silk, covered with lace and little teeny-tiny pearls."

"And a hat?"

"Definitely a hat," Evelyn assured her.

"And gloves?"

"If you want."

"What color?"

"Pink?"

"How about blue?"

"Pale blue?"

Alexandra shook her head. "Sapphire blue?"

Derek laughed. "Where does she learn this stuff?"

"The Home Shopping Channel," Evelyn told him.

Then, without warning, Alexandra crawled up on Derek's lap and gave him a big hug and kiss. "I miss my daddy," she told him, "but I'm glad you're going to be my substitute daddy."

Evelyn wasn't as surprised by Alexandra's statement as she was by the tears in her fiancé's eyes.

"You're still going to go through with this, aren't you?"

"Yes, I am."

Michael's disapproval came through loud and clear. "Then I think you'd better brace yourself," he recommended. "You're probably not going to be on Earth long enough to say 'I do.'"

"Let me talk to the Boss," Derek pleaded.

"I'm afraid that's not possible."

"Why not? I'm an angel."

"You're an angel on probation," Michael pointed out.

"But you could talk to—"

Shaking his head, Michael raised a hand to silence him. "That's not the way things are done here, Derek," he reminded him. "You already know that."

"There are never any exceptions?" Derek asked.

"Perhaps, but that has to be the Boss's decision," Michael told him.

"I can't ask him?"

"No."

"You can't ask him?" Derek wanted to know.

"I could."

"Well, then—"

"But I'm not going to."

"Why not?"

"Because you were warned, Derek," Michael pointed out. "You were told not to start things you wouldn't be able to finish."

"She was going to lose the kids, Michael," Derek said again. "I had to do something."

"You have no right to use Evelyn Sloan or anyone else to serve your own purposes!" Michael snapped angrily.

"Who's using her?" Derek argued.

"You are!"

"Look, when I marry Evelyn, I'm going to do everything I can to make the weeks we'll have the happiest of her life."

"*If* you have any weeks at all," Michael corrected him pointedly.

"All right, *if!*" Derek didn't bother to hide his frustration. "Look, Evelyn and the real Jeffrey were having problems before his accident. If he'd died while he was in the hospital—"

"He did," Michael reminded him.

"He did, but not as far as Evelyn knows," Derek said. "For Evelyn, this has been a second chance, a chance to correct what went wrong between them."

"So far, you haven't been doing a very good job of *that*," Michael reminded him.

"I know," Derek said, "but that's going to change."

"Why now?"

"Because I'm desperate," Derek confessed.

"Good reason."

"All right, so I'm not perfect, so I make mistakes."

"You make a lot of mistakes," Michael said.

"I make a *lot* of mistakes," Derek acknowledged. "What I'm trying to do now is correct as many of those mistakes as I possibly can."

"You really believe you can do that?"

"Yes, I do," Derek said confidently. "When my time's up, Evelyn will mourn Jeffrey, but she won't have to mourn the relationship. I'm going to make her as happy as I possibly can. I'll leave her with financial security, two great kids and a lot of good memories."

"You'd better," Michael said, his tone holding a definite warning note. "If you blow it this time, you could be permanently expelled from Heaven."

Derek didn't have to ask what that meant.

Chapter Nine

"Want to help me pick out my wedding dress?" Evelyn asked.

Sharon grinned. "Won't that make me an accessory to the crime?"

"Sharon!"

"Relax. I'm only kidding," Sharon assured her.

Evelyn shot her a look of unmasked disappointment. "I wish you could be happy for me," she said quietly.

Sharon frowned. "I wish I could be happy for you, too."

"Why can't you?"

"We've been through all of this before," said Sharon. "If we get into it now, you'll just be mad at me again, and I don't want that. So let's just drop it, okay?"

"You think I'm marrying him for the wrong reasons, don't you?" Evelyn persisted.

"I think he's marrying you for the wrong reasons," Sharon said. "I don't know about you."

"Is love ever the wrong reason?" Evelyn asked.

Sharon gave a little nod. "It can be, yes."

"How?"

"I thought we weren't going to get into this."

"I *need* to get into it, Sharon," Evelyn confessed. "I need to talk about it."

Sharon hesitated momentarily. "You're having second thoughts, aren't you?"

"No, not exactly."

"What, then?"

"Well ... it was no secret that we'd been having problems before the accident," Evelyn began. "After he came home from the hospital, he was different. Like a different person. I believed we had a chance to work things out."

"Believed? Past tense?"

Evelyn frowned. "The more time he spent with the kids, the better their relationship was," she recalled. "But the more time the two of us spent together, the more distant he became with me. It was as if he were making a concentrated effort not to feel too much for me."

"That doesn't make sense, even for Jeffrey," Sharon said.

"I know," Evelyn admitted. "But I still believe the relationship can be saved. That's why I'm going through with the wedding."

I have to find a way to pull this off, Derek told himself.

"You do, indeed."

Startled, he turned to see Michael behind him. "Don't do that!" he shrieked.

"Do what?"

"Sneak up on me like that!"

"Who's sneaking?" Michael asked. "Angels don't generally make noise. That's just the way we are, nothing I can do about that."

"What are you doing here in the middle of the day?" Derek asked, mildly annoyed by the unexpected intrusion.

"I came bearing good news," Michael announced.

"Yeah? What?"

"You've been given a second chance."

"A reprieve, huh?"

"For crying out loud, don't make it sound as if you've been in prison!" Michael snorted impatiently.

"I think my time on Earth would have been easier if I'd spent it in prison," Derek grumbled.

"As I've already said, you've been given another chance," Michael sniffed. "The Boss has decided to allow you to prove your intentions are honorable where Evelyn Sloan is concerned."

"Meaning?"

"If you make good on your promise to make the last few weeks of Jeffrey's life the happiest weeks of Evelyn's life, if you can really leave her with something good and positive, you can return to Heaven."

"And if I don't?"

"I don't think you want to know what will happen."

"It *is* beautiful," Sharon conceded.

They were in the most exclusive bridal shop in Seattle, where Evelyn had spent the morning trying on wedding dresses. The dress she had on at the moment was an off-the-shoulder, tea-length white satin, covered with sheer lace and tiny seed pearls.

"I thought this would be better than a full-length dress since it's going to be a small wedding," Evelyn told her sister.

"Intimate weddings are the best kind, I think," the bridal consultant helping her commented.

"So do I, for the right people," Sharon agreed.

"Sharon!" This was Evelyn.

"Oh, I agree," the consultant said pleasantly. "Small, intimate weddings can be beautiful, but they're not right for everyone."

"I'm sure." Evelyn made a face at Sharon.

"Is this going to be an outdoor wedding?" the consultant asked, thoughtfully scrutinizing the dress Evelyn was wearing.

Evelyn shook her head. "It's going to be an evening ceremony," she said.

"Candlelight," the older woman guessed.

Evelyn nodded.

"Lovely," the consultant proclaimed. "Positively lovely."

"I hope so."

"Oh, it will be," the woman predicted confidently.

Evelyn only smiled, wishing she were able to share that optimism, wishing she could feel the way she always thought she'd feel if and when she married Jeffrey.

She could only hope things would change after the wedding.

* * *

"I wish you could be my best man, pal," Derek told Michael as he stood in front of a full-length mirror in a small room at the church, fiddling with his tie.

"I'll always be your best man," Michael deadpanned.

Derek chuckled, shaking his head. Michael's very dry sense of humor still came as a surprise to him, sneaking up on him when he least expected it.

"Is there no one on Earth you can ask?" Michael queried.

He shook his head. "I'm still not sure who Jeffrey's friends were," he said. "I'm not even sure he *had* any friends."

"You should be able to identify with that," Michael said.

"I had friends!"

"Name one," Michael challenged.

"Well, uh . . ."

"You *had* friends," Michael said, "but you gradually lost contact with all of them after Patricia left you, as you spent more and more of your time with your children."

"They needed me."

"Of course they did," the senior angel agreed. "I wasn't condemning you, I was simply stating a fact."

"I suppose you're right," Derek said, stealing a quick glance at his watch, "but could we continue this conversation later? I have a wedding to attend."

"It's not too late to change your mind."

"Really, Sharon." Evelyn adjusted her headpiece. "I wish you could be at least a little optimistic, even a little bit happy for me."

"I could be," Sharon sniffed, "if you were marrying someone else."

"At least wish me luck."

"That I will do. You're going to need it."

"Sharon!"

"I'm a realist, Ev," Sharon said as she checked the back of her sister's dress. "I don't believe this marriage has a prayer."

"As you've said many times before."

"If I didn't care, I'd keep my mouth shut and let you find out the hard way," Sharon told her.

"Well, I guess I'm going to have to find out that way anyway," Evelyn responded with an exaggerated sigh.

"Not going to listen to the voice of reason, huh?"

Evelyn laughed. " 'Fraid not."

"Can't say I didn't try." Sharon left the room to check on the flowers that hadn't yet been delivered.

Alone for the first time since they'd arrived at the church, Evelyn stared absently at her own reflection in the mirror. She told herself she was doing the right thing, that Jeffrey wouldn't be marrying her, no matter what the reason, if he didn't really care about her. Hadn't he told her as much? Hadn't he said they'd work things out?

If only he'd said he loved her.

They hadn't invited many people. Only their closest friends and family—or, more accurately, *her* closest friends and family. He, it turned out, hadn't invited anyone. Sharon found that highly suspicious, but Evelyn wasn't at all surprised. Social as Jeffrey had always been, he wasn't really close to anyone. His so-called friendships were all on the surface, lacking in genuine emotional intimacy.

The children were there, and the joy they exhibited made both Evelyn and Derek certain they were doing the right thing.

Look at Patrick, Derek thought, watching his son with a pride more fierce than ever. He looks so grown-up in his dark suit and tie, carrying the ring on that little satin pillow, never letting on that he's afraid he's going to drop it.

Then Alexandra made her entrance, and Derek was amazed at the transformation his little tomboy had undergone. She wore a full, sapphire-blue dress covered with white lace and a matching hat that framed her face like a blue halo.

A halo, Derek thought proudly. Appropriate for my little angel.

Evelyn appeared behind Alexandra. She looked exquisite in her simple, but elegant white dress, her red hair up in a Gibson girl-style that was enhanced by her white floral headpiece. She really is beautiful—in every way, Derek thought as he watched her coming down the aisle toward him, toward a future they weren't going to have.

She deserves better than I can give her, Derek thought. She's a good woman, a wonderful woman. She's been more of a mother to my kids than Patricia ever was. She loves me—Jeffrey—more than either he or I deserve.

Evelyn took her place at his side, and what Derek saw in her eyes made him feel like the biggest cad who ever walked the earth.

I'll make it up to you, he vowed. Somehow.

* * *

I love him, Evelyn thought, looking up at the man she was about to marry. I love him, and in his own way, I know he loves me.

He's right. This is the answer for us. We'll work out our problems. I know we will.

She looked at Patrick and Alexandra. Now she could legally adopt them. Once she and Jeffrey were married, they could go to Family Services. They could begin the legal process that would make the children theirs, once and for all.

Yes, she thought, I am doing the right thing.

She scanned the faces of the people looking on. For the most part, they looked approving. Happy for her. Happy for them. Especially her mother. Of course. Her mother understood.

Then she looked at Sharon. She didn't have to guess what Sharon was thinking. She knew only too well how her sister felt. In fact, her sister's feelings about her marriage were clearer to her than were her own.

I love him, she thought.

We'll work it out, she kept telling herself.

The ceremony began. It was a very traditional ceremony. She'd suggested they write their own vows, but Jeffrey had been against it. He was no good at that sort of thing, he'd told her, maintaining that most men weren't. Evelyn suspected that he didn't want to have to write or speak his feelings for her because he wasn't yet sure exactly what they were.

"I now pronounce you man and wife," the minister was saying. "You may kiss your bride," which Jeffrey did, with unexpected tenderness.

Then they both knelt to kiss the children.

* * *

"So what do I do now?"

"What do you mean?" Michael said.

"It's my wedding night."

"So, it is."

"What am I going to do?"

"I'm afraid I don't understand the question, Derek."

"This is my wedding night. Evelyn is my wife now. She's going to expect me to, uh ... you know."

"Ah ... we're talking about sex now, aren't we?"

"You catch on fast."

"Thanks."

"So what am I going to do?"

"Don't you think you should have given some thought to this before you proposed?"

"You're no help at all."

"I'm only putting you on, Derek. There's really no problem at all."

"The—heck—there isn't!"

"There isn't. You and Evelyn are married now. It's all right to perform your husbandly duties—unless of course, you're physically unable—"

"Funny as a crutch, Michael."

"Now, morally—"

"Let's leave well enough alone, okay?"

"I suppose."

"Now, if you don't mind ..."

"Right. Better not keep your new bride waiting."

"Thanks a lot."

"We aim to please."

"Bad choice of words."

"Sorry."

Derek opened the door, and what he saw took his breath away. Evelyn was standing by the bed, wearing only a midnight blue teddy. Her long, lush hair tumbled freely around her face and shoulders.

"You look—incredible," Derek gasped.

"Thank you," Evelyn responded, and as Derek got closer, he could see that her lower lip was trembling.

We're so formal with each other, he thought. Guess it's up to me to do something about that.

He stepped forward, taking her in his arms. . . .

Evelyn lay awake most of the night—their first as a family in Jeffrey's house—staring into the darkness, knowing she should feel something other than confusion. This was her wedding night, and physically at least, it hadn't been a disappointment. Her new husband was still a wonderful lover. He'd been passionate, yet caring and tender. He'd made love to her— really made love to her, more so than ever before.

But what are you *feeling,* Jeffrey? she wondered.

She turned to look at him, sleeping peacefully beside her, and wished she knew what the future held for them.

He opened his eyes. "What's the matter?"

She forced a smile. "Did I wake you?"

"No," he said softly. He asked again, "What's wrong?"

"Nothing. Just the excitement of the day, I suppose," she told him.

"Mmm...that's what every man likes to hear from his wife," he responded in a suggestive tone.

"Silly!" she scolded him playfully. "I said, 'the excitement of the day,' not the night—though the night wasn't half-bad, either."

"Not half-bad?" he asked. "Maybe we should take another shot at it."

Evelyn started to laugh as he pinned her down and pretended to bite her neck. "Jeffrey!" she shrieked. "Jeffrey, no!"

"Yes," he growled. "Can't have my bride describing her wedding night as 'not half-bad' now, can I?"

He was tickling her, and she was laughing so hard that tears were streaming down her cheeks. Then his mouth was on hers, and playfulness turned to passion.

"I can't sleep."

They both froze at the sound of Alexandra's voice. Derek rolled over, groaning loudly as his daughter bounded across the room and crawled into bed between them.

"We should have gone on that honeymoon your mother offered us," he told Evelyn.

"You seem more relaxed," Michael observed.

"Just getting used to my new skin," Derek insisted.

"Yours, or your wife's?"

"Crude, Michael. Very crude."

"It's the truth, isn't it?"

"Evelyn and I *are* more relaxed with each other— yes," Derek finally admitted.

Michael nodded. "I've always known sexual tension was a problem for you."

"Sexual frustration is more like it."

"There's more to it than that, though, isn't there?"

"What makes you say that?"

Michael snorted loudly. "This is me you're talking to, Derek, remember? I know what you're thinking, I know what you're feeling," the senior angel reminded him.

"That's not comforting, you know."

"I'm sure."

Derek was in his underwear, standing in front of the bathroom sink while he shaved. "What are you getting at, Michael, or do I even have to ask?"

"Why don't you just admit that you have feelings for her?"

"Why? What's to be gained by it?"

"Maybe more than you think."

"Right."

"Why *are* you fighting it?"

"Because, to paraphrase the song, only fools fall in love."

"When are you going to get past all that bitterness?" Michael asked.

"When is *it* scheduled to freeze over?"

Michael shook his head. "You've gotten off to a great start with your new wife, Derek. Don't let Patricia get in the way."

"Are we a real family now?" Patrick asked.

Evelyn couldn't hide her surprise. "Of course we are, sweetheart," she told him. "Why do you even ask?"

"Because I wasn't sure." He climbed up on a stool near the kitchen counter on which Evelyn was working. "Alexandra and me... we've never had a real family before."

"Not even when both of your parents were alive?" Evelyn asked as she chopped onions.

The child shrugged. "I guess. I don't remember."

"How much *do* you remember about your mother, Patrick?" Evelyn asked then, trying to keep her tone casual.

"Not much," he said. "She wasn't with us very long, and when she was, I don't remember her doing mother-type things with us."

"I'm sure she loved you in her own way," Evelyn said, attempting to console him.

"I don't think so."

"What makes you say that?" Evelyn asked.

"She didn't want us."

"Oh, I'm sure that's not true—"

"Yes, it is. That's why she left."

"Did your father tell you that?"

"No," the boy responded, shaking his head. "He said she left because they didn't love each other anymore, but we knew."

"Knew what?"

"That she didn't want us."

"How did you know?"

"We could tell," Patrick said simply. "She didn't do things mothers are supposed to do. She never held us or kissed or hugged us or even read us any bedtime stories. She wasn't around all that much."

"What about your father?"

"Dad was the best."

It was then that Evelyn looked up to see her husband standing in the doorway... with an odd look on his face.

Chapter Ten

In the next two weeks, the relationship between Derek and Evelyn began to change. They became that real family Patrick had spoken of to Evelyn. The kids finally had two parents who loved them and, it seemed now, also loved each other. They did things together, as a family; they went to the zoo, the amusement park, the beach, even the wrestling matches. Evelyn even developed a grudging admiration for the kids' hero, Sonny Simms.

And Evelyn and Derek did things as a couple. Romantic things. They went out to dinner at only the most romantic night spots. They went on picnics. They took long walks along the Sound. They talked about everything, from books and TV shows to their innermost hopes and dreams. Evelyn was once again amazed by the change in the man she believed was Jeffrey Callander.

"I have to admit that he does seem to have turned into a model husband," Sharon conceded. "I guess miracles do still happen."

Evelyn smiled. "He's been so loving and attentive," she confided. "Even more so than he was when we first fell in love."

"Well," Sharon began with a note of reluctance in her voice, "I have to admit that I've never seen you happier."

Coming from Sharon, the comment was of monumental importance. Sharon was a wisecracker by nature; their friends had all told her she should be a stand-up comic. But Evelyn knew those wisecracks had just been a safe way of expressing her feelings, good or bad, when they made her uncomfortable.

Like her concern for her sister.

"I just wish he'd open up more about himself," Evelyn said then.

"How so?"

"I know there's something in his past that made it difficult for him to reach this point," Evelyn said. "He had to deal with a lot of emotional garbage along the way."

"Be thankful he did deal with it," Sharon advised.

"I am," Evelyn said quickly. "I wish he'd share that with me, too."

"Have you ever told him that?" Sharon asked. "Have you ever brought it up at all?"

Evelyn shook her head. "I've thought about it a lot—I may have mentioned it once or twice when things weren't going well. Once, he implied there was something painful in his past, but he didn't want to get into it and I've never pressured him to do so."

"Maybe you should," Sharon suggested.

Evelyn thought about it. "Maybe I should," she finally agreed.

"Bedtime," Derek announced.

"Aww!" the kids protested in unison.

"Sorry, but it's a house rule," Derek told them. "Everybody under the age of ten has to be in bed by nine o'clock."

"I'm getting a fake ID," Patrick grumbled to his sister as Derek shooed them up the stairs to their bedroom.

"Don't you guys think it's about time you agreed to separate rooms?" Derek suggested as he tucked them in.

"Not yet!" Alexandra protested.

"She's afraid of the dark," Patrick explained.

Derek didn't remember his daughter ever being afraid of the dark. "Since when?" he wanted to know.

"Since our dad died," Patrick told him. "She's afraid of a lot of things, but mostly of being alone."

Derek sat down on the edge of Alexandra's bed. "You don't have to be afraid, honey," he told her. "What happened to—your daddy, well, that was an accident. He didn't want to leave you. Nobody really wants to die. Just because Pat or Evelyn or I might have to leave you from time to time doesn't mean we're not coming back."

"My daddy didn't come back," she told him.

How he wished he could tell her! "In a way, Lexi, your daddy will always be with you," he said finally.

She gave him a puzzled look.

"In here," he said, pointing to her heart.

She smiled. "That's what Evelyn told me."

"It's true, you know."

* * *

"They're finally asleep," he announced as he descended the stairs.

Evelyn smiled. "You were up there awhile," she noted. "They must have really put up a fight this time."

He was silent for a moment. "Alexandra told me I could be her daddy until her real daddy comes back for her."

Evelyn frowned. "They really miss him," she said as Derek sat down on the couch next to her.

"I've noticed. His death must have been a major blow to them." He put his arm around her.

She put her head on his shoulder. "From what I've seen, and what Family Services told me, it was traumatic."

"They seldom mention their mother, though."

"No, they don't talk about her much." She looked up at him. "But then, neither do you."

"What?" He was stunned.

"In all the time I've known you, Jeffrey," she began, pulling herself upright, "I can't remember you ever saying much of anything about your mother, or your father."

He gave an inward sigh of relief. For a minute there, he thought she'd seen through him—literally. "There's not much to tell," he said evasively.

"It must be terribly painful for you if you can't talk about it at all," she said sympathetically.

"I never said I couldn't talk about it," he responded. "There's nothing to tell, that's all."

Her eyes met his. "Please don't shut me out, Jeffrey—not now, when things are so good between us."

He hesitated for a long moment, remembering what he'd read in the diaries and gathered from Michael. "All right," he said, taking a deep breath. "There is more to it. A lot in my past is still a blank but I remember some things."

"Tell me, Jeffrey," she urged. "Share it with me."

He nodded. "You're right," he said finally. "I should have told you a long time ago."

She said nothing, waiting for him to go on.

"My parents split when I was very young."

She nodded. "You've already told me that."

He nodded, too. "I was pretty much ignored by both of my parents after their split," he went on, hoping he was getting his facts straight. "It was a bitter, messy divorce, but I got the worst end of it."

"I'm sorry," she said softly.

"I was the most miserable kid on the face of the earth," he told her. "I promised myself I'd never be in that position again. The only way I thought I could be sure of that was never to get married, never let myself fall in love."

She was thoughtful for a long moment. "I'm glad you changed your mind," she said finally.

"That's why I wouldn't let myself get close to the kids," he said.

She looked up, confusion written all over her face. "I don't—" she began.

"When a marriage breaks up, the kids always get the worst end of it," he said quietly. "It's the kids who are hardest hit by divorce."

"But—"

"I never expected us to last, Ev," he said. "I figured if the kids didn't like me, if I never got close to them, they wouldn't much care if I was suddenly out of the picture."

"What changed your mind?" Evelyn asked.

What indeed? he wondered. Aloud he said, "Coming so close to death has a tendency to make one reconsider one's priorities."

"You seemed confused at first," she recalled.

"I was." That much, at least, was true.

"It might have helped if we'd talked about it before," she told him.

"Maybe," he said, nodding. But he was thinking, I doubt it. What would I have said? Sorry I've been such a louse—and by the way, I'm not really Jeffrey Callander?

"At least we're talking about it now."

"Yeah." And I've got *both* feet in my mouth.

"Really getting into the part now, are we?"

"Funny, Michael. You're a regular stand-up comic," Derek grumbled as he reorganized the contents of the desk in his study.

"The domestic role does seem to agree with you," Michael pointed out.

"I *was* a single father before I—died—remember?"

"My memory is perfect," Michael sniffed. "And I'm quite aware of your previous mortal status."

"Aw, now don't go getting all bent out of shape on me," Derek told him. "You were the one who started it, after all."

"I didn't start anything," the senior angel responded. "I merely made an observation."

Derek smiled slyly. "Sometimes I get the feeling you're trying to act as my conscience," he said.

Michael shrugged. "It's a dirty job, but someone has to do it, I suppose," he said with a heavy sigh.

"Funny. Real funny."

"You *do* seem more—dare I say it?—satisfied," Michael persisted.

"Why does that surprise you?" Derek questioned. "The more I learn about Jeffrey, the more comfortable I am with the role."

"Are you sure you don't mean you're more comfortable the better you get to know *Evelyn?*" Michael wanted to know.

Derek shook his head. "You never give up, do you?"

"Being able to read minds has its advantages."

"Seems like forever since we've been here," Evelyn commented.

About two weeks later they were having dinner at Canlis on Aurora Avenue, their favorite restaurant in the early days of their relationship. As it had been then, Evelyn reflected, she was having seafood while her husband had ordered steak.

"Some things never change," she commented.

"Huh?"

"We used to eat here at least once a week."

He nodded, somewhat hesitantly, as if not sure how she expected him to respond.

"I always ordered seafood and you always ordered steak."

He nodded again.

"We seem to be in a rut."

He laughed, a laugh of puzzling relief. "So it would seem."

"Maybe we should make an effort to change."

He shrugged. "What for?"

"I don't know. I just don't want us to ever become bored with each other," she admitted.

He smiled. "I can only speak for myself," he said, "but I could never be bored with you."

She gave him a skeptical look. "I think you *were* bored with me, and not too terribly long ago," she said.

He shook his head. "It wasn't you."

"Wasn't it?"

"No, it wasn't. Why don't you believe that?"

She pursed her lips thoughtfully. "I've been told I've become something of a drag," she confided.

He looked genuinely surprised. "Who told you that?" he asked.

"Sharon, actually."

"Your sister?"

She nodded.

"The one I've never gotten along with?"

"I only have one sister, Jeffrey," she reminded him.

He grinned. "Sometimes not being able to remember can be a blessing," he told her.

Evelyn smiled. "She wishes she could forget you, too," she admitted.

"So, what did she say to you to make you think you could be a drag?" he wanted to know.

"She told me I wasn't any fun anymore."

"Did she get specific?"

Evelyn thought about it for a moment. "She said I used to be a party animal, that I used to be happier and more cheerful."

"To what does she attribute the alleged change?" he asked.

She hesitated. "You and the kids," she said finally.

"How does she figure that?"

"She thinks I've turned into a real sitcom mom—you know, car pools, bake sales and the PTA." She paused. "She said the problems between you and me had robbed me of my sense of humor."

His eyes met hers. "Do you believe that?" he asked.

"No, of course not."

"Are you sure about that?"

"Yes, I'm sure," she insisted. "Why do you ask?"

"We've had a lot of problems. *I've* had a lot of problems," he reminded her, as is she needed to be reminded. "I've had a lot of old emotional baggage to deal with, and I know you've suffered because of it."

"Maybe for a time, but not now," she told him. "You're dealing with it. *We're* dealing with it."

"I'm trying," he corrected.

"I'll help, if you'll let me," she said.

"Sometimes I wonder if anybody can help me," he said with a hint of sadness in his voice.

"Give me a chance," she urged.

Give us a chance, she was thinking.

Derek had a *big* problem.

Hard as it was to admit, even to himself, he was falling in love with Evelyn.

How had this happened?

He hadn't thought it was possible, not for him. Hadn't Patricia left him immune to love? Hadn't he learned his lesson the first time around?

Obviously not.

Of course, Evelyn was nothing at all like Patricia. Evelyn was warm and caring and giving and spontaneous. Patricia was selfish and cold and unfeeling, a woman who cared only about herself, her own needs and wants.

Evelyn made him feel good about himself; Patricia had made him feel like a failure as a husband and as a man.

Evelyn taught him to enjoy life, to live it to its fullest; Patricia had made him wonder why he even bothered.

Evelyn was unlike any woman he'd ever known.

Yes . . . Derek had a *big* problem.

Chapter Eleven

"You're going to do *what?*"

"You heard me, Michael," Derek stated flatly. "I'm going to tell Evelyn the truth."

"As in 'the whole truth and nothing but the truth?'"

"You got it."

"You can't! It's out of the question!"

Derek wasn't backing down—not this time. "Look, I don't care what happens to me—okay, maybe I *do* care what happens to me—but I owe her this," he insisted. "I've made a mess of things, I've made a mess of her life. I owe her the truth."

"It's against the rules!"

When Derek turned to face Michael again, there were tears in his eyes. "I'm not going to say I'm not scared," he began carefully. "I am. I never knew I could be so scared. But I can't just go away one day without any kind of explanation, without telling her the truth."

"I've already told you what the consequences will be if you break the rules," Michael reminded him.

"I remember," Derek said, "but this is something I have to do."

Long after Derek had returned to Earth, Michael continued to think about Derek, about his predicament, about their conversation. Derek did have a chance. He had one shot at salvation, but in Derek's case it was a long shot at best.

Evelyn, I'm not who you think I am.

Terrific, Derek thought. Open with a line like that, and she'll think I'm some fugitive from the law who had my face redone to look like Jeffrey's.

Remember when you asked me if I wanted to be the kids' father? Well, I am.

No good. She'd just think I'd flipped.

Do you believe in the Hereafter?

No...sounds like the lead-in for an infomercial.

There was no easy way to tell her this. He was just going to have to get to the bottom line right off the bat and put all of his cards on the table. And hope she didn't have him hauled off to the nearest funny farm.

Maybe I should feel her out on this first, he considered. Find out what she believes and doesn't believe in. Maybe she believes in angels.

Maybe she believes in miracles.

But would she believe in those things the way they had actually happened?

"How come we're staying at Betty's tonight?" Patrick wanted to know.

"I'm really not sure, sweetheart," Evelyn answered honestly. "Jeffrey said it was going to be a surprise. That's all I know."

"I like surprises," Alexandra chirped.

"Me, too," Patrick agreed enthusiastically.

Evelyn only smiled.

"I hate to disappoint you guys, but I think the surprise is for me," she told them.

"Oh."

"Rats!"

"Well, I like that," Evelyn said with mock anger in her voice, keeping her eyes on the road as she drove them to her mother's home across town. "You two are always getting presents and surprises, but now that it's my turn, you don't like it?"

"I'm sorry," Patrick said, eyes cast downward.

"Me, too," said Alexandra.

Evelyn laughed. "It's okay, kids," she assured them. "I'm not mad, I was just kidding."

"What's the surprise?" Alexandra asked.

Evelyn smiled. "Well, now, it wouldn't be a surprise if I knew what it was, would it?" she asked.

"I guess not," Patrick conceded.

"Is it a good surprise?" Alexandra asked.

"Silly!" Patrick scolded. "All surprises are good."

"No, not all of them," Evelyn told him.

He gave her a quizzical look. "You mean there are *bad* surprises, too?"

"Unfortunately, yes," she answered truthfully. "Some surprises are downright unpleasant."

"Is that the same as bad?"

"Absolutely."

"Could Jeffrey's surprise be a bad one, then?"

Evelyn wished she knew.

* * *

"So what's the big surprise?"

Startled, Derek turned to face Evelyn. "I didn't hear you come in," he said, struggling to regain his composure.

"I could tell," she said, nodding. "Your thoughts were a million miles away. At least."

"Something like that, yeah," he admitted.

"So what's the surprise?" Evelyn asked again.

He hesitated. "It's not a surprise, exactly," he said finally.

"I see."

"It's just something I have to share with you. Something we have to talk about," he told her, unable to conceal his uneasiness.

"Sounds ominous." Evelyn seated herself on the couch. "You know, on the way to my mother's, I was trying to explain to the kids the difference between a good surprise and a bad surprise."

"And?"

"I have the distinct feeling that what we have here is going to be a bad surprise."

"Not bad," he told her. "Just incredible. It's going to be very hard to believe, if not impossible, but I swear, with God as my witness, that it's the truth."

"The suspense is killing me," she said, trying to keep her voice light. "What is it?"

"I don't even know where to start."

"The beginning would be a good place," she suggested.

"Even that won't make this any easier to swallow."

"Jeffrey, you're making me very nervous with this," she said then. "Will you just get to the point?"

"All right." He swallowed hard, hoping lightning wouldn't strike. "I'm not who you think I am."

"You're not." It was more of a statement than a question.

"No."

"You're not Jeffrey Callander?"

"No."

"Okay, I'll bite. Who are you?"

He frowned. "You don't believe me."

"Frankly, no. But I'll play along anyway," she told him. "Who are you?"

"Derek Wolfe."

It didn't register at first. "Who—oh, wait a minute." Her eyes widened in disbelief. "Wolfe—the children's father?"

"That's me," he said lamely.

"Right. And I'm the Tooth Fairy."

"I realize this is hard for you to believe—"

"No, it isn't hard for me to believe—it's impossible for me to believe!" she snapped angrily. "I don't know why you're doing this, Jeffrey, but it's really sick. Derek Wolfe died almost nine months ago."

"Yes, he did."

"You need help," she told him.

His eyes met hers. "Do you believe in the Hereafter, Evelyn?" he asked.

"Do I believe in what?"

"The Hereafter—you know, God, Heaven, angels—"

"Of course I believe in God!" Evelyn snapped. "What has that got to do with this?"

"I told you, I'm Derek Wolfe."

She shook her head. "What are you saying? That you, Derek, have come back from the dead?"

"Something like that, yes."

"Something like that?"

"I'm an angel."

"An angel. I see," she said, nodding slowly. "And where, may I ask, are your wings?"

"There are no wings on my Earthly body."

"Jeffrey's body."

He nodded. "Jeffrey's body."

"O-kay." She looked at him as if he'd lost it. Which, of course, she must have thought he had. "And *how* did you come into possession of Jeffrey's body?"

"He died," Derek said simply.

"He died."

"Are you going to keep repeating everything I say?"

"I'm trying to come up with a logical reason for what's happening here." She was suddenly pale.

"It's really quite simple."

"Sure it is. One of us—or maybe both of us—is losing it in a very big way."

"No."

"No? Then what?" she asked. "Am I supposed to believe that my fiancé—Jeffrey Callander—is dead and that you're some sort of reincarnation of Derek Wolfe?"

"You're half-right."

"Enlighten me."

"Jeffrey is dead. He died in all the ways that matter while he was in that coma," Derek said.

"In all the ways that matter?" She stared at him incredulously. "What's that supposed to mean?"

"It means that his soul had left his body."

"They said he was brain-dead," she remembered. "They said the machine kept his body alive. They said it was a miracle he—you—came back."

"Jeffrey Callander didn't come back. Derek Wolfe did," he said solemnly.

"I have to give you credit," she said with a hollow laugh. "You have an incredible imagination."

"This isn't a fantasy," Derek insisted. "It's reality."

"You'll excuse me if I ask for proof."

"Proof? It's proof you want? All right." He orally listed everything he knew about Derek and Patricia Wolfe and their children, things only the real Derek Wolfe would know.

Evelyn wasn't convinced. "You could have obtained that information in any one of a number of ways," she maintained. "It doesn't prove you're Derek Wolfe back from the dead."

"Look, I know this all sounds pretty incredible, but I swear it's all true."

"If it is, and I'm not saying that I believe for a moment that it is, why would Derek Wolfe be here now? Why would he want to marry a woman he doesn't even know?" she asked.

"That should be obvious."

"Oh?"

"The kids."

"What about them?"

Derek frowned. "I wanted to make sure they were in good hands." He paused. "My former wife was not a good mother. After the kids were born, she decided she didn't really want to be a mother, and didn't bother to try to hide her dissatisfaction. Finally our marriage fell apart and she walked out."

"That's what the social worker told me," Evelyn recalled.

"I was the product of a broken home myself, so I had a pretty good idea of what they were going through," he said. "My parents split when I was young. My mother used to say she'd found the one person in the universe who was put on this earth just for her, and they'd proceeded to put each other through five years of sheer—well, you get the picture."

Evelyn nodded.

"I don't remember much about that time, when we were all together under one roof," he continued. "Just the fighting, and there was almost never a cease-fire. Mom said I was an early crawler—I guess that was my survival instinct at work. I was going for cover." He paused. "I swore when I got married, it would be different. I thought Patricia wanted the same things I wanted, but I guess I was wrong."

Evelyn said nothing, waiting for him to go on.

"I was a single father with two small children," he said. "It wasn't easy, but it *was* a labor of love. The kids had problems—they were insecure because of their mother's rejection—but we were very close. After my death, I worried that they would end up with the wrong kind of person or persons. I worried that they'd be frightened, that they'd have problems again. I got permission to come back, to make sure they were all right."

Evelyn was shaking her head. "You got permission to come back," she repeated slowly.

He nodded.

"This is unreal."

"My superior, Michael, he's one of the senior angels—"

"Angels?"

He nodded again.

"You're telling me you're an angel?"

"A novice angel, actually," he responded.

"A novice angel," she echoed. "And this Michael—"

"He's a senior angel, my supervisor," Derek told her. "He got the Boss to let me come back."

"An angel supervisor, the Boss—you make the Hereafter sound like the AFL-CIO," she declared.

"Not exactly," he said with a tired smile.

"So the—Boss allowed you to...uh, come back. Then what?" she wanted to know.

"He gave me sixty days."

"Sort of like a weekend pass."

"I'm serious."

"So am I."

"Once I had permission to return," he continued, "I had to find a body to inhabit. Michael and I went to the hospital. Finding Jeffrey there was a stroke of luck."

"Luck!"

"I didn't mean it the way it sounded," he said quickly. "But for me it *was* a stroke of luck. What better way to get close to you and find out what kind of life you'd made for my kids than becoming your fiancé?"

"Husband," Evelyn corrected.

He nodded. "Husband."

Her eyes met his. "If this were true, why would you marry me?" she questioned.

"So you could get permanent custody of the kids," he answered. "*Legal* custody."

"You said you got permission to come back for sixty days?"

He nodded.

"What happens at the end of that sixty days?"

"I'm not sure."

She gave him a quizzical look.

"The original plan was for me to come here, make sure the kids were healthy, happy and secure, and return to Heaven."

"That's changed?"

"Maybe."

"Why?"

"I broke the rules."

"What rules?"

"It's a long story," Derek said evasively. "But what it boils down to is this, I screwed up big-time, so I may not be allowed to go back."

"You'll stay here, then."

He shook his head. "I'll be heading for a warmer climate," he said grimly. "Much warmer."

"What about Jeffrey?"

"I told you, he died."

"Obviously his body didn't."

"It will, when I leave it."

"It will just . . . die."

"That's pretty much it."

She stood up. "Right."

"You do believe me, don't you?"

Evelyn sighed heavily. "I believe you need help, Jeffrey," she told him. "I believe something happened to your brain when you were down there without oxygen."

"This is the truth!" he protested.

"I believe you believe that." She started for the door.

"Where are you going?" he asked anxiously.

"To get the kids. And then back to my house."

"For good?"

"I don't know yet. Right now I'm not sure about anything, Jeffrey," she said truthfully.

And she walked out.

He was scaring her.

Evelyn couldn't stop shaking. As she drove to her mother's, her hands trembled on the steering wheel. What could have done this to him? What could have caused his wild delusions?

Angels, indeed!

Did he really expect her to believe such an incredible tale? Of course he does, she thought miserably. He believes it. He really believes he's Derek Wolfe, that he's come back from the dead, that he's living here in Jeffrey's body while he checks up on his children.

What else does he believe?

Hadn't the doctors warned her this could happen? Hadn't they told her his brain had been deprived of oxygen for a very long time, that there could be permanent damage?

They *hadn't* told her he might go insane.

She wondered if he could be dangerous. Maybe she should keep the children away from him. She decided it was probably a good thing she hadn't sold her own house when she and Jeffrey married. She was probably going to need a place to live.

You should be ashamed, she scolded herself. Didn't you vow to love him "in sickness and in health"? You claim to love this man, yet as soon as you realize he's ill, you're ready to bail out, turn your back on him!

What kind of wife are you?

Well, you really blew it this time!

Derek paced the floor like a caged animal. Alone in the darkness in the master bedroom, in which he would be sleeping alone tonight, he tried desperately to think of a way to repair the damage he'd done, ironically, by being totally honest with Evelyn.

"That was a stupid thing to do, Derek."

"Michael?"

"Of course."

"Jeez—where were you when I needed you?"

"I beg your pardon?"

"She didn't believe me."

"Yes, I know."

"You were there?"

"Of course."

"Why didn't you show yourself, then?"

"Show myself?"

"Yeah, you know, materialize. Show her I was telling the truth."

"You know that's not allowed, Derek."

"But—"

"As you are already aware, you were doing this without the Boss's blessing, if you'll pardon the expression. You cannot expect any Divine intervention on your behalf, under the circumstances."

"But—"

"You broke the rules, Derek."

"But I did it with the best of intentions."

"You know what they say about good intentions."

"Does that mean I'm not coming back to Heaven?"

"I don't know yet."

"When, then?"

"Don't call us, we'll call you."

Evelyn didn't know what to do.

"I think he's lost it, Mom," she told Betty Sloan as they sat at Betty's kitchen table, drinking coffee well into the night while Betty patiently listened to Evelyn's concerns.

"He's been through so much," Betty reminded her daughter. "Could it be that the stress is taking its toll on him?"

"No doubt," Evelyn said, shaking her head sadly. "I wish I knew what to do."

"Talking to his doctors might help," Betty suggested.

"I was talking about our marriage."

Her mother looked surprised. "You're considering divorce?" she asked.

"I don't know what I'm going to do yet, Mom." She sighed. "I just don't feel like our marriage has a chance."

"Has he changed that much?"

Evelyn's smile was sad. "At first I thought all the changes were going to be for the better," she recalled. "He was so warm and giving, he was trying so hard, I was sure everything was going to be all right. Then he started doing so many strange things, and now this..." Her voice trailed off.

"I repeat, talking to his doctors might help."

Evelyn decided it couldn't hurt. Things couldn't possibly be any worse between them than they were now.

* * *

I've got to do something, Derek thought, growing more frantic by the minute.

"Don't you think you've done enough already?"

"Michael?"

"Of course."

"Materialize, will you?"

"No can do."

"Why not?"

"I think you already know the answer to that, Derek."

"Right. I'm in deep—"

"Don't say it."

"Why? What have I got to lose?"

"Maybe more than you think, Derek."

"Has the Boss made a decision yet?"

"In a way."

"Meaning what?"

"Meaning that, for the moment, you're on probation."

"For how long?"

"That's up to Him."

"How do I go about redeeming myself, then?"

"I can't tell you that."

"Can't or won't?"

"Can't. You have to find it within yourself."

"What's that supposed to mean?"

"You *are* a novice. Reach into your own soul, Derek. Reach deep within your soul."

"I hate riddles."

"It's no riddle, friend. You just have to find what's already there."

"'Find what's already there,'" he repeated aloud, no longer sensing Michael's presence. "If that's not a riddle, I don't know what is."

Reach into your own soul.

And find what? he wondered.

Reach deep within your soul.

What's usually within the realm of the soul? Emotions? Feelings?

"Love," he said aloud.

But love for whom? The kids? He didn't have to reach deep into his soul for that. It was there, sure, but not only down deep. It was there at the surface, too, for all the world to see.

Not the kids, no.

If not the kids, then who?

Evelyn?

Yeah, that made sense.

Michael had always thought Derek was in love with Evelyn, right from the beginning. How many times had he tried to get Derek to admit it?

Hogwash!

Or was it?

What *did* he feel for Evelyn, really? He felt something, he couldn't deny that. But what? He wasn't sure himself.

Love?

No, that wasn't possible.

It wasn't possible because he wouldn't allow it to be possible. He would never again open himself up to that kind of pain.

Still . . .

He thought about it. He thought about his kids...about Evelyn ...about the things Michael had said...about what he felt and the fate awaiting him if he didn't face all of those feelings. Impulsively, he reached for the phone.

"Evelyn . . . we have to talk."

Chapter Twelve

"We have nothing to talk about."

"You don't mean that."

"Right now I do," she said stiffly.

"Right now?"

"I need time, Jeffrey."

"Derek."

"Jeffrey," she repeated emphatically.

"Have it your way," he said in surrender. "You don't believe me."

"Do you blame me?" she wanted to know.

"You told me you believed in God, in the Hereafter—"

"Not the way you described it!"

"Okay, so it's not what you were taught in Sunday school," he conceded. "Did it ever occur to you that you'll get a different version depending on which Sunday school you go to?"

"None like yours, I'll bet."

"How can anyone really know what it's like until they've been there?" he challenged.

"No one's ever come back to tell about it," she said pointedly.

"*I've* come back!"

"Jeffrey, I love you—I can't help that—but I can't deal with this," she told him. "You need help—help I can't give you."

She hung up. Derek sat there for a long moment holding the receiver.

"I need you, Evelyn," he said finally.

I need you, Jeffrey.

Evelyn stared at the telephone, more than once tempted to pick it up and call him back, but she didn't. She couldn't. As much as she loved him, right now she was afraid of him. He wasn't himself. He'd definitely changed. The changes in his personality were difficult enough to deal with. The delusions were impossible.

He believed them. He really believed he'd returned from the dead. He wasn't just putting her on.

The phone rang then. Evelyn let it ring, knowing the answering machine would pick it up. It did, and she listened to Jeffrey's voice, begging her to pick up. Twice she almost did. She reached for the receiver, but withdrew both times. She couldn't. Not now.

Maybe never.

He called back four times over the next two hours, but Evelyn never picked up the phone, never spoke to him, much as she would have wanted to.

Please, God, she silently prayed, tell me what to do.

"I thought you weren't allowed to be seen with me," Derek said sarcastically.

"Careful, there," Michael warned. "You're going to blow it if you don't learn to control that mouth of yours."

"Blow what?"

"The Boss is reconsidering your probationary status," Michael told him.

"Is that good news or bad news?" Derek asked cautiously, not sure he wanted to hear the answer.

"In this case, it's good news," Michael assured him.

"How so?"

"He's considering lifting the probation," Michael explained.

"So, I'll be recalled soon," he concluded.

"You don't sound very happy about it," Michael noticed. "I thought you'd be relieved."

"Well, yeah, I guess I am," he said without much enthusiasm.

"Want to talk about it?"

"What?"

"Whatever it is that's bothering you."

Derek hesitated at first, then nodded. "It's Evelyn," he said finally. "You were right."

Michael nodded. "I know."

"You know? But how could you—" He stopped short. "What am I thinking? Of course you know."

"You don't want to leave her," Michael stated.

Derek shook his head. "No."

"Do you remember what I told you?"

Derek nodded. "Only too well," he said. "You said if I could learn to open myself up to another human being completely, to love and be loved totally, I'd have a shot at staying on here."

Michael nodded.

"I don't suppose two out of three counts," Derek said miserably.

"The lady still won't talk to you, then?"

"The lady won't even answer her phone."

"Does this surprise you?"

Derek gave a heavy sigh. "No. I suppose not," he said, regretting his mishandling of the situation.

"I'll see what I can do," Michael promised.

Evelyn slept fitfully.

This is a dream, she told herself. It has to be. She was flying—no plane, no wings, no wires, no nothing. Just flying, floating really, hundreds—no thousands—of feet above Earth, pulled by a force she couldn't see or feel, through the clouds to an incredible place so beautiful, words couldn't begin to adequately describe it.

Heaven. It had to be Heaven.

She was greeted at the gates by a funny-looking little man with shaggy hair and a beard, dressed in torn, faded jeans, a Save the Earth T-shirt and bare feet. "Welcome to Paradise," he greeted her.

"This is Heaven?" she asked.

He nodded.

"And you are—"

"You may call me Michael," he told her. "I'm one of the Boss's senior angels."

"The Boss?"

He lowered his voice reverently. "You know... Him."

"God?"

"The One and Only," he answered.

"And you're an angel?"

"That I am. You seem surprised," he noticed.

"Well," she began, more than a little embarrassed, "you're not exactly—"

"I don't look like what you expected an angel to look like," he guessed.

Evelyn flushed. "Well, no," she admitted.

He only smiled. "This will come as a surprise to a lot of people, but to God we are *all* beautiful," he told her. "What you on Earth have seen of angels is nothing more than an artist's rendition."

"Why am I having this dream?" she asked him then.

"It's not a dream," he said patiently. "You're having an out-of-body experience, Ms. Sloan."

"No," she said, shaking her head emphatically. "This is a dream. It had to be a dream. It's because of Jeffrey, isn't it?"

"Derek," he corrected.

"He's not Derek Wolfe. He can't be!" she insisted. "Derek Wolfe is dead!"

"So am I," he told her.

"Am I losing my mind?" she asked, near tears.

"Not at all," he said reassuringly. "You're here because Derek tells us you've been a hard sell."

"A what?"

"A hard sell. You didn't believe him when he elected to tell you the truth," Michael said.

"Would you?"

"Of course I would, but then our positions are hardly the same," he pointed out.

"Why?" she asked. "Even if all of the things he told me were true, why did he tell me? Why did he have to tell me anything at all?"

"Because he's fallen in love with you."

"*What?*"

"He's in love with you," Michael said again. "Derek was worried about his children after his death. They'd already suffered so much because of their mother's rejection, he was naturally concerned that their foster mother be the right kind of person."

"He *was* checking me out?"

"Exactly."

"But why didn't he just, you know, visit me, like the ghosts in *Topper?*"

"He's not a ghost, Ms. Sloan," Michael reminded her. "He's an angel."

"There's a difference?" Evelyn asked.

"Oh, yes, a big one."

"Go on," she urged.

He nodded. "The availability of your fiancé's body was a fluke," he told her. "Jeffrey had just joined us—"

"Jeffrey's in Heaven?"

"Yes."

She laughed aloud. "This is some dream. If Jeffrey, scoundrel that he is—was—made it to Heaven, there's hope for everyone."

"Ms. Sloan!"

"Look, Mr.—"

"Michael."

"Michael—I loved Jeffrey Callander, but I didn't wear blinders where he was concerned, no matter what my sister thinks. I knew better than anybody that he was no saint," she told him.

"Did you know how much he loved you?"

She laughed again. "That's the one thing I wasn't sure about," she admitted.

"He does, you know."

She gave him a quizzical look. "How do you know—"

"I told you, he's here."

"But you said—"

"I said he died by Earthly standards. The spirit is eternal," he explained.

"He made it to Heaven. That's wonderful."

Michael smiled. "Derek Wolfe was also a bit of a scoundrel," he confided, "but he was an exceptional father. He loved his children. That's the most important thing, you know."

Evelyn looked at him, not sure she understood.

"Love," he told her. "No matter what else one had done with his or her life, if one has given of themselves fully and completely, that's the main thing."

"Are you telling me Jeffrey loved me like that?"

Michael nodded.

"I never had a clue."

"I don't think that was such a good idea," Derek told Michael later.

"What?"

"Telling her about Jeffrey."

"She asked. What would you have had me do, lie to her?"

"Well, yeah."

"Derek!"

"Look, I love Evelyn. If there's a chance, even a long shot, that I can have a future with her, I want that chance," he said. "But she's already confused about her relationship with Jeffrey. She was confused about it when I went back. This is only going to make her more uncertain."

"But it's you she married," Michael pointed out. "It's you she's been with these past weeks."

"In Jeffrey's body."

"It's still your soul."

"It still has to be confusing for her," Derek argued. "No matter *who's* on the inside, it's Jeffrey on the outside. How's she supposed to forget what she can see with her own eyes?"

"If you really love her, you'll convince her," Michael said.

Derek snorted loudly. "Thanks for making my job a hundred times harder."

"Job?"

"Figure of speech."

Michael nodded. "At least now she doesn't think you're nuts," he pointed out.

"Are you sure about that?"

I must be nuts, Evelyn thought.

It had to be either a dream or a hallucination. Either way, it would seem she definitely had a problem.

She sat up in bed. It seemed so real, but it couldn't have been. It wasn't possible was it? Could she have really visited Heaven? Could that funny-looking little man really have been an angel? A senior angel?

Could Derek Wolfe really be living in Jeffrey's body?

Jeffrey. If only she could believe what the "angel" had told her about Jeffrey. She wanted more than anything to believe it. She wanted to believe that he had really loved her, that whatever his reasons for not letting her know it, his feelings for her were as deep and as real as hers for him.

"It had to be a dream," she said again, this time aloud. But as she got out of bed, she caught sight of something on the nightstand that stopped her cold.

It was a gold medallion, a very unusual gold medallion, unlike anything she'd ever see before.

Except in her dream.

"You told me once that Jeffrey could end up with permanent brain damage as a result of his accident," Evelyn began, hoping that by the time she finished, the doctor wouldn't think *she* had suffered permanent brain damage.

The doctor nodded. "I said that, yes," he began, "but having examined him thoroughly, not once, but several times since he came out of the coma, I can say with certainty that he's suffered no permanent organic damage."

"What about behavioral changes?"

He eyed her cautiously. "Could you be more specific?" he asked, concern in his voice.

"Personality changes. Hallucinations. Delusions."

"What's he done?"

"It's not so much what he's done as what he believes." Evelyn drew in a deep breath. "He thinks he's an angel."

The doctor didn't try to hide his surprise. *"What?"*

"He thinks he's an angel," Evelyn repeated. "He says Jeffrey died in the hospital and he took over Jeffrey's body."

"And who does he think he is if he's not Jeffrey Callander?" the doctor asked.

"Derek Wolfe," Evelyn said. "Wolfe died several months ago. He was the father of the two children I'm trying to adopt."

"I see." The doctor was silent for a long moment. "Has his behavior toward the children changed in any way?"

"Dramatically," she answered. "When the children first came to live with me, Jeffrey wanted no part of them. He wasn't interested in fatherhood. But after the accident, after he came home, everything changed. He adored the children, couldn't spend enough time with them. In fact, for a while there, the kids were seeing more of him than I was."

The doctor nodded. "Well, Ms. Sloan, I'm not a psychiatrist, but it seems to me that Jeffrey has experienced an overwhelming sense of guilt where the children are concerned and is attempting to make it up to them."

"So he really does know he's Jeffrey Callander?" Evelyn wanted to know.

"I can't be sure without talking to him myself, of course—but it sounds as if he does, yes."

Evelyn thought about the doctor's words as she left the office and waited for the elevator that would take her to the underground parking garage. Could he be right? she wondered. Digging down into her pocket, she took out the medallion she'd found on her nightstand.

She wished she knew.

"Evelyn's not here."

Sharon spotted Derek the minute he came into the restaurant and was prepared to head him off at the pass.

"I know she's not here," Derek told her. "I came here to talk to you."

"Now what could we possibly have to talk about?" she asked coldly.

"I can think of one thing," he offered. "Evelyn."

"What about her?"

"She talks to you."

Sharon frowned. "Not as much as you and the world at large might think," she admitted.

"How much has she told you?" he wanted to know.

"About what?"

"Don't play games with me, Sharon," he growled. "This is too important."

"Who's playing games?"

"How much has she told you?" he asked again, making it clear he wasn't about to drop the issue.

"All I know is that she moved out," Sharon said, annoyed with him and not bothering to hide it. "I figured she must have finally come to her senses."

"I love her, Sharon."

"You have a funny way of showing it."

"There's a lot you don't know."

"I'll bet."

"I'm serious, Sharon."

"So am I."

"There's been a lot wrong between Evelyn and me, a lot she couldn't understand," he admitted, "but I love her and I want to make things right between us."

"Excuse me if I don't believe you."

"I don't care if you believe me or not!" he exploded.

Sharon stepped backward, stunned by his angry outburst. "Look, she—she doesn't talk to me about your problems," she stammered. "She doesn't tell me anything because she knows what I think of you. I guess she figures I wouldn't be objective."

"When she does come in," he said as he started for the door, "tell her I have to talk to her."

"Tell her yourself."

"I would, if she'd take my calls."

Derek decided he was going to have to resort to drastic measures.

"What are you doing here?" Evelyn asked as she got out of her car.

It was dark and raining hard, but Evelyn had seen Derek, leaning against her garage door, even before she'd pulled into the driveway. She was reluctant to even get out of her car.

"We need to talk."

"You need to see a doctor."

"You didn't even believe Michael."

She froze. "Michael?"

"I know he paid you a visit, or rather he arranged for you to pay him a visit," he said.

She stared at him in disbelief. "How did you know about my dream?"

"It wasn't a dream."

"Of course it was a dream. I—"

He shook his head. "Not a dream," he said gently. "It was an out-of-body experience."

"How do you know so much about it?"

He managed a slight smile. "I told you, Michael's my senior angel. He did this as a favor to me, to help me convince you I've been telling the truth, that I really am who and what I say I am."

"Describe Michael," Evelyn challenged.

He didn't hesitate. "Short, scruffy, looks like he could use a haircut. Hair and beard are brown, eyes are blue. He usually wears sandals or no shoes at all,

ratty jeans and slogan T-shirts. Loves slogan T-shirts,"
he said. "Oh, and he wears glasses—the small square
kind that were popular back in the sixties."

Evelyn's eyes widened in disbelief. "How did
you—"

"I told you, it was no dream."

Evelyn had trouble absorbing the reality at first.
"You're not Jeffrey?"

He shook his head. "No."

"But you're living in Jeffrey's body?"

"For now, yes."

"So the man I married isn't the man I thought I
married."

"That's basically it."

She drew a deep breath. "Is the marriage legal?"

He smiled. "Since I *am* Jeffrey Callander, as far as
this world is concerned, anyway, I would have to assume that it is, yes."

She gave a little laugh. "Well, I certainly can't con-
sult a lawyer about it, can I?" she asked.

"I wouldn't."

Then she frowned. "You told me you'd only been
given sixty days on Earth," she remembered.

He nodded.

"Your time's almost up, then. But Michael's trying
to help you—"

"He knows how much I love you."

She stared at him, suddenly speechless.

"He knew what I felt for you even before I did,"
Derek told her. "Because of my experience—my very
negative experience—with my ex-wife, I've tried very
hard *not* to love you. Even when Michael pointed out
that I could have more than my allotted sixty days,
that I could have a second chance here on Earth, if I

could open myself to love, if I could love and be loved completely."

"Then there's no problem."

"Unfortunately, there is," he disagreed. "Halfway doesn't count."

"Halfway?"

"I love you, Evelyn, but you don't love me."

"But I do," she insisted. "As much as I loved Jeffrey, there was always a kind of wall between us. Michael said Jeffrey loved me, but it wasn't enough. I grew up with two parents who loved each other and loved my sister and me unconditionally. They were always there for us, and that's the way it should be. Sharon and I may have been as different as Kool-Aid and beer, but we were still close—we *are* still close— because that's the way we were brought up. Jeffrey couldn't understand that, I guess because his own childhood was so different. I thought he'd changed after we were married, but now that I know the truth, I know the man I loved, the man I was so happy with, was really *you,* Derek."

"Do you mean that?"

"I've never meant anything more in my life."

"It's funny," he began. "Jeffrey and I came from pretty much the same kind of background, yet I grew up wanting something better, while he was always afraid to reach out."

"Maybe you just had a level of courage he couldn't achieve—at least not emotionally."

"I don't know," Derek said, shaking his head. "Maybe it was the circumstances of our respective parents' marriages that made the difference."

She gave him a puzzled look. "What do you mean?"

"My parents fought all the time—but as hard as that was to take, I suspect Jeffrey's parents' indifference toward each other would be a lot worse—at least for a kid."

"You talk as if you know something about it," she noticed.

"I do."

"How?"

"Michael told me."

"You talked to him—about us?" she asked.

He nodded again. "He told me as much as Jeffrey loved you, he'd never been able to get past his doubts and fears."

Evelyn frowned. "Maybe he just didn't love me enough," she said quietly.

His eyes met hers then. "Well, *I* do."

She smiled. "You really mean that, don't you?"

"I've never meant anything more."

"I'm glad . . . because I love you, too."

"Me—or Jeffrey?"

"*You.*"

"*That's all I needed to hear,*" said a disembodied, but familiar voice.

"*Michael?*"

"*Who else? I bring good news from the Boss.*"

"*My probation's been lifted?*"

"*Better than that. You've got that second chance you wanted.*"

"*Really?*"

"*I don't joke about such things, Derek.*"

"*No, of course not.*" He held Evelyn close. "Will you marry me?"

She laughed. "We're already married, silly."

"So we are." He kissed her. "So we are."

Epilogue

"Where are we going?" Derek gave his wife of six months a puzzled look.

"Can't tell you," Evelyn said with a mischievous grin. "That would ruin the surprise."

"Give me a hint, then."

"Nope."

"Not even a little one?"

"Uh-uh."

"Maybe I'm not dressed for the occasion—"

"What you're wearing is just fine," she assured him.

"Are we going someplace here in Seattle?" he continued to pressure her.

"I'm not telling you anything," she said firmly, ushering him into a waiting limousine.

"Well, at least tell me what the occasion is, then," he urged.

"You'll find out soon enough," she promised, producing a black cloth blindfold.

He resisted at first. "Oh, no, you don't!"

"Don't ruin it, Wolfe," she warned.

"Do you think that's a good idea?" he asked as she secured the blindfold. "Calling me by that name, I mean?"

"It is your name," she reminded him.

"Yes, but—"

"You look like Jeffrey," she told him, "but now that I know who you really are, I can't think of you as anyone but Derek Wolfe."

"That'll be a little hard to explain to the world at large," he pointed out.

"Oh, to everyone else you'll always be Jeffrey," she conceded. "It's that, or the funny farm for us."

"Doesn't sound even remotely appealing." He chuckled.

Evelyn laughed, too. "I think anyplace would be appealing as long as we're together," she told him.

"Such a romantic!"

"Would you want me any other way?"

"I'd want you any way I could get you," he said seriously.

"Yeah, right!"

The car came to a stop. "Are we there?"

"Not quite," she answered evasively. "But we do have to get out of the car."

"Why? Does it turn back into a pumpkin at midnight?" he asked.

"Maybe."

"Come on, Evelyn—"

"Don't spoil it, Derek," she warned, leading him up a flight of stairs. "This is the most special, most important night of our lives."

"We got a tax refund!"

"Dream on."

"Sharon's buying you out."

"Sure, and next week, we're going to part the Red Sea," she said with a touch of sarcasm in her voice.

"I believe that's already been done."

"So it has."

A pause. "When are you going to tell me?"

"Soon enough. Now sit down."

He obeyed, and had the nagging feeling he was on a plane. Not the standard commercial airliner, but a smaller craft. Maybe a Learjet. So, they weren't having dinner in Seattle. Must really *be* a special occasion, he decided.

But what?

It didn't seem to Derek that they'd been in the air that long when the aircraft began its descent. Evelyn still wouldn't allow him to remove his blindfold, but promised she'd do so very soon.

Before he knew it, they were on the ground and in a car again, headed for God-only-knew-where. "This had better be worth it," he told Evelyn in a mock-warning tone.

"It will be."

"Michael?"

"You know someone else who communicates with you this way?"

"I didn't think I'd ever hear from you again. I mean, now that I'm no longer, uh, one of you."

"You'll always be one of us. And you will be back, when your time comes."

"Again."

"Again."

"So I will hear from you, even now?"

"Missed me, did you?"

"Oh, come on!"

"You did. Admit it."

"Okay, so I did. Big deal!"

"It is a big deal, Derek. It shows you genuinely care for others."

"That surprises you?"

"Yes, it does."

"So what's Evelyn's big surprise?"

"Sorry, pal. You'll just have to wait until your wife's ready to tell you. I'll be in touch."

"Time for the unveiling," Evelyn announced.

When she removed the blindfold, he realized they were in front of the Donatello Hotel—in San Francisco!

"We're having dinner at the Donatello," she told him.

Inside the hotel's restaurant, they were escorted to one of the private dining rooms. "I'm impressed," Derek told Evelyn as wine was served.

"As you should be," she said with a sly smile.

"You still haven't told me the reason for all this."

"And I'm not going to. At least not yet."

"Why all the secrecy?"

She smiled. "You'll see—"

He raised a hand to silence her. "I know. Soon enough."

"Right."

It was an impressive outing, he decided as dinner was served. She'd gone to a lot of trouble. Whatever this surprise of hers was, it had to be something big.

"Are you going to keep me in suspense all night?" he asked over dessert.

Her eyes twinkled. "You won't have to wait much longer," she promised.

"That's what you keep telling me," he said, trying to hide his amusement. He wanted her to think he was angry, but he didn't think she was buying it.

"Believe me, it will be worth the wait."

"So you've said." As the wine steward refilled his glass, he noticed hers. "You've barely touched your wine," he commented.

She shrugged. "I'm not much of a drinker."

"I didn't know."

"Of course you didn't."

"Jeffrey did."

"But you're not Jeffrey."

He drew in a deep breath. "It's such an incredible relief to not have to pretend—at least not with you—to be Jeffrey anymore."

"I'm glad you told me," she said. "For a while there, I thought I was losing my mind."

"You? Never!"

"I was beginning to wonder."

He paused. "Do you think we'll ever be able to tell the kids—who I really am, I mean?"

"Maybe someday, but not anytime soon," she said. "They're too young. They might be able to understand their father's come back—children are much more open to that sort of thing than adults are—but they wouldn't be able to understand why they couldn't tell anyone."

He nodded. "I guess you're right."

"You're disappointed."

"Well, sure I am. My death brought them a lot of pain. I'd love to be able to tell them I've come back to them."

"Someday," she promised. "Besides, we have other news to break to them when we get home."

He opened his mouth to ask her what she was talking about when their waiter returned, placing a covered silver tray in front of him. "What's this all about?" he asked.

Evelyn smiled mischievously. "Why don't you lift the lid and find out?" she suggested.

He did. There was no food on the tray, just a tiny pair of knitted booties. It took a moment to register; then his eyes widened in disbelief. "Does this mean what I—I think it means?" he stammered.

She nodded, beaming. "I'm six weeks pregnant."

He jumped up, rushing to embrace her. "I can't believe it," he said, kissing her, tears of joy streaming down his cheeks. "I didn't think—under the circumstances I wasn't sure I could—"

She laughed. "It's true," she told him. "Miracles do still happen."

*   *   *   *   *

MILLION DOLLAR SWEEPSTAKES (III)

No purchase necessary. To enter, follow the directions published. Method of entry may vary. For eligibility, entries must be received no later than March 31, 1996. No liability is assumed for printing errors, lost, late or misdirected entries. Odds of winning are determined by the number of eligible entries distributed and received. Prizewinners will be determined no later than June 30, 1996.

Sweepstakes open to residents of the U.S. (except Puerto Rico), Canada, Europe and Taiwan who are 18 years of age or older. All applicable laws and regulations apply. Sweepstakes offer void wherever prohibited by law. Values of all prizes are in U.S. currency. This sweepstakes is presented by Torstar Corp., its subsidiaries and affiliates, in conjunction with book, merchandise and/or product offerings. For a copy of the Official Rules send a self-addressed, stamped envelope (WA residents need not affix return postage) to: MILLION DOLLAR SWEEPSTAKES (III) Rules, P.O. Box 4573, Blair, NE 68009, USA.

EXTRA BONUS PRIZE DRAWING

No purchase necessary. The Extra Bonus Prize will be awarded in a random drawing to be conducted no later than 5/30/96 from among all entries received. To qualify, entries must be received by 3/31/96 and comply with published directions. Drawing open to residents of the U.S. (except Puerto Rico), Canada, Europe and Taiwan who are 18 years of age or older. All applicable laws and regulations apply; offer void wherever prohibited by law. Odds of winning are dependent upon number of eligibile entries received. Prize is valued in U.S. currency. The offer is presented by Torstar Corp., its subsidiaries and affiliates in conjunction with book, merchandise and/or product offering. For a copy of the Official Rules governing this sweepstakes, send a self-addressed, stamped envelope (WA residents need not affix return postage) to: Extra Bonus Prize Drawing Rules, P.O. Box 4590, Blair, NE 68009, USA.

SWP-S594

IT'S OUR 1000TH SILHOUETTE ROMANCE, AND WE'RE CELEBRATING!

JOIN US FOR A SPECIAL COLLECTION OF LOVE STORIES BY AUTHORS YOU'VE LOVED FOR YEARS, AND NEW FAVORITES YOU'VE JUST DISCOVERED. JOIN THE CELEBRATION...

April
REGAN'S PRIDE by **Diana Palmer**
MARRY ME AGAIN by **Suzanne Carey**

May
THE BEST IS YET TO BE by **Tracy Sinclair**
CAUTION: BABY AHEAD by **Marie Ferrarella**

June
THE BACHELOR PRINCE by **Debbie Macomber**
A ROGUE'S HEART by **Laurie Paige**

July
IMPROMPTU BRIDE by **Annette Broadrick**
THE FORGOTTEN HUSBAND by **Elizabeth August**

SILHOUETTE ROMANCE...VIBRANT, FUN AND EMOTIONALLY RICH! TAKE ANOTHER LOOK AT US! AND AS PART OF THE CELEBRATION, READERS CAN RECEIVE A FREE GIFT!

YOU'LL FALL IN LOVE ALL OVER AGAIN WITH SILHOUETTE ROMANCE!

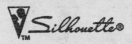

CEL1000

Get set for an exciting new series from
bestselling author

ELIZABETH AUGUST

Join us for the first book:

THE FORGOTTEN HUSBAND

Amnesia kept Eloise from knowing the real reason she'd
married cold, distant Jonah Tavish. But brief moments of sweet
passion kept her searching for the truth. Can anyone help Eloise
and Jonah rediscover love?

Meet Sarah Orman in *WHERE THE HEART IS*. She has a way
of showing up just when people need her most. And with her
wit and down-to-earth charm, she brings couples together—
for keeps.

Available in July, only from

Silhouette
R O M A N C E™

WILD RIVER

by
Laurie Paige

Maddening men...winsome women...and the untamed land they live in—
all add up to love! Meet them in these books from Silhouette Special Edition
and Silhouette Romance:

WILD IS THE WIND (Silhouette Special Edition #887, May)
Rafe Barrett retreated to his mountain resort to escape his dangerous feelings
for Genny McBride...but when she returned, ready to pick up where they
left off, would Rafe throw caution to the wind?

A ROGUE'S HEART (Silhouette Romance #1013, June)
Returning to his boyhood home brought Gabe Deveraux face-to-face
with ghosts of the past—and directly into the arms of sweet and loving
Whitney Campbell....

A RIVER TO CROSS (Silhouette Special Edition #910, September)
Sheriff Shane Macklin knew there was more to "town outsider"
Tina Henderson than met the eye. He saw a generous and selfless woman
whose true colors held the promise of love....

Don't miss these latest Wild River tales from Silhouette Special Edition
and Silhouette Romance!

SEWR-4

Join award-winning author Marie Ferrarella as she kicks off her new series,

BABY'S CHOICE

in May with
**CAUTION: BABY AHEAD,
SR#1007**

City slicker Shane Michaels had returned to rustic Wilmington Falls on impulse—and he was *not* a spontaneous man. Country doctor Jeannie Harrigan, too, had been acting quite impetuously. And when their carefully guided paths crossed, their destiny was undeniable—and made in heaven.

Share the wonder of life and love, as angelic babies matchmake the couples who will become their parents, only from

Silhouette
ROMANCE™

It's our 1000th Silhouette Romance™, and we're celebrating!

And to say "THANK YOU" to our wonderful readers, we would like to send you a

FREE AUSTRIAN CRYSTAL BRACELET

This special bracelet truly captures the spirit of CELEBRATION 1000! and is a stunning complement to any outfit! And it can be yours FREE just for enjoying SILHOUETTE ROMANCE™.

FREE GIFT OFFER

To receive your free gift, complete the certificate according to directions. Be certain to enclose the required number of proofs-of-purchase. Requests must be received no later than August 31, 1994. Please allow 6 to 8 weeks for receipt of order. Offer good while quantities of gifts last. Offer good in U.S. and Canada only.

And that's not all! Readers can also enter our...

CELEBRATION 1000! SWEEPSTAKES

In honor of our 1000th SILHOUETTE ROMANCE™, we'd like to award $1000 to a lucky reader!

As an added value every time you send in a completed offer certificate with the correct amount of proofs-of-purchase, your name will automatically be entered in our CELEBRATION 1000! Sweepstakes. The sweepstakes features a grand prize of $1000. PLUS, 1000 runner-up prizes of a FREE SILHOUETTE ROMANCE™, autographed by one of CELEBRATION 1000!'s special featured authors will be awarded. These volumes are sure to be cherished for years to come, a true commemorative keepsake.

DON'T MISS YOUR OPPORTUNITY TO WIN! ENTER NOW!

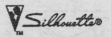

CELOFFER

CELEBRATION 1000! FREE GIFT OFFER

ORDER INFORMATION:

To receive your free AUSTRIAN CRYSTAL BRACELET, send three original proof-of-purchase coupons from any SILHOUETTE ROMANCE™ title published in April through July 1994 with the Free Gift Certificate completed, plus $1.75 for postage and handling (check or money order—please do not send cash) payable to Silhouette Books CELEBRATION 1000! Offer. Hurry! Quantities are limited.

FREE GIFT CERTIFICATE   096 KBM

Name:_____

Address:_____

City:_____ State/Prov.:_____ Zip/Postal:_____

Mail this certificate, three proofs-of-purchase and check or money order to CELEBRATION 1000! Offer, Silhouette Books, 3010 Walden Avenue, P.O. Box 9057, Buffalo, NY 14269-9057 or P.O. Box 622, Fort Erie, Ontario L2A 5X3. Please allow 4-6 weeks for delivery. Offer expires August 31, 1994.

PLUS

Every time you submit a completed certificate with the correct number of proofs-of-purchase, you are automatically entered in our CELEBRATION 1000! SWEEPSTAKES to win the GRAND PRIZE of $1000 CASH! PLUS, 1000 runner-up prizes of a FREE Silhouette Romance™, autographed by one of CELEBRATION 1000!'s special featured authors, will be awarded. No purchase or obligation necessary to enter. See below for alternate means of entry and how to obtain complete sweepstakes rules.

CELEBRATION 1000! SWEEPSTAKES
NO PURCHASE OR OBLIGATION NECESSARY TO ENTER

You may enter the sweepstakes without taking advantage of the CELEBRATION 1000! FREE GIFT OFFER by hand-printing on a 3" x 5" card (mechanical reproductions are not acceptable) your name and address and mailing it to: CELEBRATION 1000! Sweepstakes, P.O. Box 9057, Buffalo, NY 14269-9057 or P.O. Box 622, Fort Erie, Ontario L2A 5X3. Limit: one entry per envelope. Entries must be sent via First Class mail and be received no later than August 31, 1994. No liability is assumed for lost, late or misdirected mail.

Sweepstakes is open to residents of the U.S. (except Puerto Rico) and Canada, 18 years of age or older. All federal, state, provincial, municipal and local laws apply. Offer void wherever prohibited by law. Odds of winning dependent on the number of entries received. For complete rules, send a self-addressed, stamped envelope to: CELEBRATION 1000! Rules, P.O. Box 4200, Blair, NE 68009.

 ONE PROOF OF PURCHASE

                                               096KBM

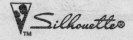